P9-DFN-718

PEACEMAKER: CONQUISTADOR'S GOLD

PEACEMAKER: CONQUISTADOR'S GOLD

•

Clifford Blair

AVALON BOOKS
NEW YORK

PRINTED IN THE UNITED STATES OF AMERICA
ON ACID-FREE PAPER
BY HADDON CRAFTSMEN, BLOOMSBURG, PENNSYLVANIA

This book is dedicated
to our dear friends
Jerome and Irene Walton.
The real "gold" in life is
knowing people like you.

Chapter One

James Stark saw the faint trace of dust rising in the distance against the late afternoon sky. He straightened from fastening the corral gate to gaze at it in silent speculation. A frown etched his forehead, and he tilted his Stetson back slightly and squinted against the glare.

One horse, he decided, being ridden hard out on the main road, concealed from sight by the rolling grasslands studded with trees. He wondered what would make a person drive a horse like that in this heat. An amateur, or a fool, he surmised, to mistreat good horseflesh like that.

Or else someone hounded by a frantic desperate need.

His gaze flicked automatically to the Winchester 1887 lever-action shotgun leaning against the fence before shifting back to that enigmatic plume of dust.

There. The answer to the single rider's haste. A larger cloud of dust—at least four horses—had risen up now in the wake of the first. Four horses ridden just as hard as that of the rider they pursued, for such it undoubtedly was—a pursuit.

The afternoon air was still, a rarity for Oklahoma Territory with its near perpetual winds, and the humid heat was heavy as the two plumes of dust hung against the cloudless sky.

His newly acquired horse farm with its stately frame house, corral system, and barns was some three miles outside of Guthrie, and he wondered if the distant chase had originated in the territorial capital. If so, the horses of both the pursued and the pursuers would be on their last legs.

The first trace of dust had disappeared now, which meant that the lone rider had stopped or, more likely, turned off the main road onto the grassy track leading to Stark's spread.

He didn't wait any longer. He clicked his tongue in that certain way, and Red, his big sorrel stallion, tossed his head and trotted over to him. He'd just turned the horse into the corral, but Red only snorted a mild protest and allowed Stark to slip the bit between his square yellow teeth.

"Sorry about this, fella," Stark said. "Looks like we're not quite done for the day."

He hefted the saddle and blanket from the corral fence and dropped them on the horse's back. They'd spent a good part of the day surveying his herd, but the ride had not been strenuous and Red was in good enough shape to carry him out to the road. Besides, it was quicker than catching another horse, and a strong sense of urgency was beginning to gnaw at him.

Red seemed to sense that urgency. The horse didn't try to swell up on him, so he got the cinch secure the first time. He glanced toward the road. Both clouds of dust had dissipated, which meant pursued and pursuers were now on the track to his spread. It could even mean that the pursuit was over, and that the pursuers had caught up to their prey. He snatched the Winchester from where it leaned against the fence and swung up into the saddle.

Red hit a gallop, and Stark felt that familiar surge of excitement at sitting on a good piece of horseflesh. Red's combination of brains, stamina, and agility was one of the reasons he had decided to start breeding horses. Prudence was the other reason. A married man had to begin thinking about settling down.

Thoughts of his beautiful wife were prominently in his mind as he reined the stallion off the track before cresting the first rolling hill. He would not allow that gnawing sense of urgency to dampen the wariness that had become so much a part of his nature. He pulled the Winchester free and moved Red forward at a trot.

He saw the cluster of riders down in the grassy draw between two hills. Even before he could make out the details, the alignment of the situation was obvious. Four of the riders had drawn their horses into a close circle around the fifth. His hunch had been right. The pursuers had cornered their prey.

Such was the intensity of the confrontation below him that none of the participants were aware of his presence. He halted his horse and studied them.

The four were of a type that was all too familiar to Stark. Hardcases. Hired guns. All of them cast from the same mold—handguns strapped low, attired in store-bought clothing any working cowhand or farmer would have disdained save maybe for a social.

Stark's hackles rose as he took in the scene, and his grip tightened on the shotgun. Trouble. Men of this ilk were bred to it and spawned it, often by their very presence. A disappearing breed, but still given to haunting the smaller disreputable towns in the area surrounding Guthrie. And just now this crew was intent on the kind of trouble they could inflict on their victim.

The fifth rider, their prey, was a woman.

Stark felt a distinct shock as he realized this, but there was no denying the long blond hair beneath the stylish Stetson, nor the trim figure clad in white blouse and divided riding skirt. She set the horse like an old hand, shifting it expertly with pressure of legs and reins to avoid the hands, which reached out to grasp her mare's bridle.

"Just hold on there, missy," the leader's voice carried clearly to Stark. "Me and the boys just want to have a little fun. You may as well enjoy it too." His laughter was harsh, crude.

The two riders at her flanks had crowded in close so that her horse collided with theirs as she tried to back away. At the same moment, the bearded leader kicked his horse forward and leaned far out of the saddle in a lunge that let one hand clamp onto her reins.

"Hah! Gotcha, missy!" His shout of triumph was exultant as he straightened in the saddle.

Stark's shot clipped the man's battered felt hat neatly from his head. The girl's horse jerked back at the report, pulling the reins from the bearded man's grasp as he fought to manage his own mount. Stark put heels to Red and hauled him out of his downhill sprint some twenty feet from the group as they brought their horses back under control.

The girl, he noted with approval, had seized the opportunity to break free from her circle of captors. She reined her mare around to face them as Stark levered the shotgun and centered it on the bearded man's chest.

"Right there, boys." His voice and the metallic click of the Winchester froze their belated grabs for their own weapons. His appraisal of them had not been in error. They were hardcases, and not particularly good ones at that.

"You're making a mistake, cowpoke," said the bearded man, whose snarl twisted his lips.

"No," Stark said flatly. "The mistake was yours. Now get out of here."

"This ain't any of your business," another one blustered.

"You're on my land. Besides, it's any God-fearing man's business when scum like you mistreat a woman." The outermost rider tried to sidle his horse clear, and Stark swung the shotgun toward him. "You, there, stay close."

"Who the blazes do you think you are?" the leader demanded.

Stark shifted the Winchester back to him. "Name's James Stark," he said flatly. He felt his mouth pull as of its own accord into that hunter's grin he had thought was fading of late. He felt the customary satisfaction at the sudden spark of fear that flared into the bearded man's eyes.

"I—I didn't know. He didn't tell us . . . That is, I'm sorry."

The man who had tried to move clear glanced over sharply. "What the devil's got into you, Al?"

"You heard him!" Al snapped back. "That's James Stark, the Peacemaker."

"That don't mean nothing to me," replied the thin, sallow-faced youth insolently. "You're acting like a no-account, yellow-bellied—" The argument with his cohort was meant as a distraction. As he spoke his hand stabbed fast for the pearl-handled .45 revolver tied low at his side.

It was an easy shot. Stark almost had a dead drop. He

swiveled the barrel of the Winchester, and in the last possible instant shifted the alignment of the shot from the gunman's heart to his shoulder before pulling the trigger.

Red stood rock steady beneath him at the blast. The slug smashed the gunman's shoulder socket, sent him reeling back almost out of the saddle as his horse shied at the report.

Stark swung the shotgun traversing across the other three. "Anyone else?"

There were no takers. Al's bearded face was pale, his hands raised well clear of his sidearm. Likewise, the other two were unwilling to follow their wounded comrade's lead.

"All right. Get out of here, and take him with you." Stark didn't use the gun to gesture. Taking his sights off men like them, even for an instant, was a fool's play.

They rode out, one of them leading the wounded man's horse. Stark waited a moment, keeping his gaze on their retreating backs, then lifted the Winchester again to his shoulder. He heard the girl gasp an instant before he pulled the trigger.

The would-be molesters' speed increased sharply at the sound of the shot. He glanced over at her as he lowered the gun.

She looked relieved. "You shot high."

"Just a reminder to keep them moving." He sheathed the shotgun. "Surprises me a mite that you'd be concerned about anything that happened to them."

"I couldn't let you shoot them down from behind!"

She couldn't very well have stopped him, Stark reflected, but didn't speak the thought aloud. It was a nice sentiment, though, and it went well with the girl who had expressed it.

She had an oval face, flushed now with excitement,

and even features that went beyond prettiness, but didn't quite touch beauty. There was a certain strength in the set of her chin and in the competent manner in which she sat on her horse.

She broke the awkward silence. "You're the man they call the Peacemaker?"

He nodded. "That's right."

"The marshal in Guthrie said you might be able to help me." The words came out in a breathless rush. "I was on my way here to see you when I saw them behind me. I knew I shouldn't let them catch me, and I tried to outrun them, but they—" Abruptly the color drained from her face and she swayed slightly, her hand tightening convulsively on the saddle horn.

Stark started his horse forward to catch her, but she seemed to recover and straightened.

She managed a weak smile. "I guess I'm a little more shaken than I thought."

"That's understandable. That was a rough crew." The words seemed inadequate, but she was obviously bearing up all right now. "Let's go on up to the house. You could probably use some coffee."

She reined her horse around, and they set off at a walk. "I'm Sarah Walker, by the way," she said, as if suddenly realizing she hadn't introduced herself. "Thank you for the rescue. I'm glad you showed up when you did."

"So am I. I'm surprised you stayed ahead of that gang for that long. You're obviously no stranger to sitting on a saddle."

She seemed pleased by the compliment. "My family vacationed out West a few times when I was growing up, and I learned to ride Western style then. I've never forgotten. Besides, back home I rode a lot, even though it was English style at the hunt clubs."

Curiosity as to the motive for her visit prodded Stark, but he kept silent. There was plenty of time, and she had been through an ordeal.

"I'm sorry to intrude this way," she went on. "I checked first at your office in town, and they said you wouldn't be in today. The secretary offered to make me an appointment for tomorrow, but the matter I need to discuss is very urgent." She glanced over her shoulder in the direction her attackers had taken. "I felt it was too dangerous to wait."

"Well, it sure turned out your feeling was accurate." Stark was hoping she'd go on into the "urgent matter," but she didn't. He reminded himself once more there was no hurry.

After a moment, he continued companionably. "You said you stopped by my office. Did you meet my wife?"

"Yes. She gave me directions out here. She said to tell you she planned to be home early."

So the mysterious Sarah Walker had piqued Prudence's curiosity as well and prompted her to change her plans. When she left this morning for the office they shared in Guthrie, she'd told him she would be working late. Until a few moments ago, he'd intended to get cleaned up and meet her in town for a late supper at one of the fancy restaurants there.

Sarah seemed to feel the same obligation he did to make conversation. "Your wife is a lovely woman. There aren't many lady lawyers around."

"Especially in Oklahoma Territory," Stark agreed.

"You two seem an unlikely match," she ventured. "I mean, a professional troubleshooter and a female attorney."

"Yep," Stark said dryly. "It seemed like that to us too." He couldn't control the grin that curled the corners of his mouth. "We fought against it as long as we could."

His attempt at humor prompted an answering smile. He was relieved to see a little of the tension drain out of the girl. He admired her grit, but he had a hunch the four gunmen he'd run off were only the first of many threats swirling around her.

They'd reached the point in the road where his large four-square farmhouse was visible at the top of the hill. It sat, solid and majestic, with white columns supporting the wraparound porch. Sarah's eyes widened a little as she saw it. Stark himself sometimes had that same reaction. The whole spread was pretty impressive.

"Did you and Mrs. Stark build the house?" Sarah asked tentatively.

"No, it was built by a federal judge sent out here from Washington to oversee the settlement of the territory. Turns out frontier life didn't set too well with him or his wife, so they went back East. Being a lawyer, Prudence heard about him leaving early on, and we were able to pick up the place for a song."

"How fortunate for you."

"Yeah, and it came along at a real good time. Me and Prudence both lived in apartments in one of the hotels in town before we were married. Things got a little confined when we moved in together. This setup gives us lots of elbow room."

"I can imagine. It's a beautiful place. How many acres?"

"A hundred and sixty—a whole section. We've got enough land that I decided to try my hand at raising horses. For years I've thought that if you took some of the fancy horses bred back East for speed and crossed them with the tough agile mustangs and Indian ponies out here you'd have almost the perfect horse."

She indicated Red. "Did you raise him?"

"Naw, I traded an Indian brave out of him when he was just a colt. He's as surefooted as any Indian pony I've ever seen and has the stamina of a wild mustang. But I don't know where he got his size from. He's quite a bit bigger than most Indian stock."

"Sounds like your perfect horse all right." The smile she flashed him wasn't genuine. He sensed the nervousness and fear in her roiling just below the surface.

Dutifully he continued the small talk. "Yeah, he's everything you'd ever need in a horse. I bought a dozen or so mares from a couple of horse farms in Maryland and Virginia to breed to him. Come spring we'll have a pasture full of his foals. If they're anything like their sire, the bloodline will catch on fast."

They rode on past the house to the barn, and handed the horses over to a stablehand. Stark had hired a couple of men to tend the stock during his frequent absences. Likewise, Prudence had found a woman to cook and clean the house. The bigger place required more time and upkeep than either of them could give with their careers. More expense too, but it was worth it. They both earned enough in their respective professions to afford a little luxury in this new phase of their lives.

Once they were settled in the comfortable lounge chairs on the front porch, Stark offered coffee again. Sarah refused that offer, but accepted some lemonade. Inez, the heavyset stoic mestizo housekeeper, quickly served them and retreated.

There were still some hours of daylight left, but the shadows were lengthening. Stark felt the stiffness from a hard day in the saddle begin to ease out of him as he stretched out his legs and sipped the cool sweet liquid. Off to the east some of his high dollar broodmares were grazing on a slope.

A pair of hawks drifted lazily overhead. Stark glanced over at Sarah. She caught his eye and sighed.

"It's so nice here," she said softly. "Peaceful. I'm sorry I showed up and ruined your day off. I suppose the least I can do is tell you why I came to see you."

"Okay, I'm listening." Reluctantly Stark eased himself up straighter in his chair. Then his eyes fell on the buggy making its way up the grassy track toward the house. He put up a hand to stop Sarah before she continued. "As anxious as I am to hear your story, I guess you better wait till my wife gets here to begin. She's nosey as all get out these days about the jobs I take. It'll save us both a lot of time and breath if we don't have to go over everything twice."

Sarah smiled at the touch of humor in his voice and nodded understanding.

He stood and walked out to meet Prudence as she stopped the buggy at the barn. Dutifully the same stablehand appeared to give her a hand down and take charge of her rig.

As usual, the mere sight of her was enough to make Stark's breath catch in his throat. Her long black hair was pulled primly back into a bun, as befitted a professional woman competing in a man's world, and she wore a simple white blouse with a high collar and a long gray skirt. But even the severe hairstyle and prim outfit couldn't hide her beauty. He was one lucky man, he told himself for the millionth time.

She waved a greeting to Stark and started up the path to meet him, a lovely smile enhancing her classic features and warming her dark eyes.

"Hi, there, Mrs. Stark. What happened to working

late at the office?" With a teasing grin, he bent to give her a peck on the cheek.

A similar merriment danced in Prudence's eyes as she answered. "Oh, I wrapped up my legal research in record time today. It's amazing how visions of one's husband with another beautiful woman can spur one on."

He slipped a possessive arm around her waist and pulled her close as they continued up the path to the house. "Now, now," he resumed the teasing, "you have no more reason to be concerned than I do knowing you're in the courtroom day after day with all those fancy legal types."

She gave him a sharp jab to the ribs and a warning frown that didn't quite reach her eyes. "Will you stop it and behave! You know Sarah's watching, and you're going to embarrass us all."

Stark glanced toward the porch and saw that indeed their playful interchange hadn't escaped the girl. She rose somewhat awkwardly and waited as they mounted the porch steps.

Prudence immediately put her at ease. "Sarah, it's nice to see you again. I'm relieved you made it out here okay. I'm never quite sure I give adequate directions."

Sarah returned her warm smile. "Oh, your directions were quite clear. I did have some trouble, but it wasn't because I got lost or anything."

Prudence glanced questioningly at Stark, but he put her off with a shake of his head. There was no need to upset Sarah again by recounting the incident. "I'll fill you in later," he said quickly. "Right now Sarah's going to tell us about her reason for looking me up."

He took Prudence's elbow and urged her into the chair beside him. Inez appeared as if by magic with another glass of lemonade and left the pitcher this time.

When Stark had refilled Sarah's glass and his own, he turned expectantly toward the girl.

She hesitated a moment, seeming to gather her thoughts, then plunged ahead nervously. "It's quite a fantastic tale really. I hope you'll listen to it with an open mind. It involves lost treasure, intrigue, and someone very dear to me." Tears welled into her eyes at that point, but she fought them down. "Do you know the story of the treasure in the Lost Cave with the Iron Door?"

Chapter Two

Stark had heard most of the tale, or variations of it, over the years. But he sat and watched Sarah as she repeated it, noting the mingled excitement and fear warring in her eyes as she spoke.

"Well, according to legend," she began, "during the early seventeen hundreds, a lucrative gold mining operation existed in the Wichita Mountains south of here long before this became Oklahoma Territory. Supposedly the mines were run by the last remnants of the greedy Spanish conquistadors who explored the Southwest in earlier times looking for treasure."

"I've heard that story," Prudence said excitedly. "The conquistadors are said to have enslaved the local Indians and forced them to work in the mines. If I'm remembering correctly, though, a number of the tribes ultimately joined forces and drove the invaders from the mountains."

"That's right." Sarah took up the story again. "In their hasty retreat, the Spaniards were unable to take the gold they'd mined with them. They engineered rockslides to cover the mine entrances, and placed the

14

gold already taken from the ground in a hidden cave. The mouth of the cave was then sealed with a massive iron door, reportedly brought into the mountains from an old Spanish galleon for some unguessable reason. Before locking the door, the conquistadors ruthlessly killed the last of their slaves who had moved the gold inside. Their bodies are supposedly entombed with the treasure."

"And the gold is still there today," Stark intoned in an emotionless voice, "because the Spaniards never made it back to reclaim it and its location was lost over the years. Ingots stacked like cordwood stored there in the darkness among the bones of the dead. All that treasure behind the iron door with its massive lock long rusted shut, just waiting for someone to solve the riddle and once again expose it to the light of day."

Sarah studied him for a moment. "So, Mr. Stark, like your wife, you've heard the story before."

"Stories," Stark corrected. "Another version has Belle Starr and her outlaw gang making off with a trainload of government gold and silver. They'd already chosen a hiding place—a remote cavern in the Wichita Mountains. But Belle wanted the cave to be secure from chance discovery, so they took the door off the baggage car and hauled it into the mountains with them. They set the door in place, concealed it with rocks and brush, and split up. The gang members were killed by lawmen before they could return for the gold, and Belle herself was killed a few years ago by an unknown assailant. The secret of the cave's whereabouts died with her."

Sarah shook her head emphatically. "That version is wrong! But I gather from your tone that you don't believe either one."

"Whether I believe it or not is irrelevant. The fact

remains that the men who have believed it over the years have ended their lives broke and demented, driven crazy by the search for a treasure no one can even prove exists."

"Oh, it exists, all right," Sarah said excitedly, "and the proof exists as well. My fiance discovered it, quite by accident, I'll admit. But the discovery was legitimate. Let me explain."

Stark listened silently as she spoke. Her fiance, Timothy Rankin, was a historian at Northeast University in their hometown of New York City. A renowned scholar, he was one of the youngest men to have obtained a full doctorate at the university.

"He's always been interested in American history," Sarah spoke quickly, "particularly in the impact the old Spanish conquistadors had on our country—the settlements they established, and the exploratory expeditions they made all across the Southwest."

Stark knew that Texas and even parts of Oklahoma Territory had been crisscrossed long decades past by parties of adventurous Spaniards seeking gold and glory. Behind them they had left a few battered artifacts, and tales told and retold around campfires by lonely men.

"Timothy found something," Sarah continued, "down in the cellar of one of the university buildings in an old trunk that was part of an estate left to the college by an elderly Spanish gentleman. No one knew anything about him or where he originally came from, just that he left everything he owned to the school."

She went on to say the items had never been inventoried. They had merely been stored and forgotten. Timothy Rankin's insatiable thirst for knowledge of things past led him to the storage cellar where he discovered the trunk and went through its contents.

"He found a map," Sarah told them. "A map made of fine silk about five feet long and two feet wide, rolled up in the bottom of the trunk beneath what amounted to trash. It took him a while to decipher it, to even realize what it was, but it showed the location of a lost cache of gold behind an iron door deep in the Wichita Mountains."

Stark could see Prudence was listening intently to Sarah's story, without any of the skepticism he felt. And it did have a certain level of plausibility, he realized, as the girl went on to explain how her fiance had delved into the background of the map.

In his research, Timothy had come across a story of a nameless Mexican who had appeared for a time in Oklahoma Territory. Inside his clothing, wrapped snugly around his waist, he had always worn a wide strip of silk on which had been painted a map of the location of the fabled treasure. It was Timothy's theory that that Mexican was the college's deceased benefactor. He was never able to learn how the map came into the man's possession.

Supposedly in the 1850s a small expedition entered the Wichitas, relying on a copy the Mexican allowed to be made of the silk map after he became frustrated by his own fruitless efforts to locate the vault. Details of the expedition were vague. But despite a series of strange accidents that delayed their progress, the map reportedly led the treasure hunters to the massive iron door. When they entered the cave, they discovered the gleaming mass of gold and the skulls of those entombed with it.

"Before they could remove the treasure, they were attacked by Indians and forced to flee," Sarah finished breathlessly. "The fighting was so fierce, they believed themselves to be hopelessly outnumbered. Fearful of the coming night and the treasure's guardians, they left the mountains, planning a return expedition with more men. However, the War Between the States intervened and none of the adventurers ever mounted another search."

"I've heard the story," Stark broke in, "but the Indians in those mountain tell a different version of what drove the treasure hunters off. They think the gold is evil, bad medicine. They say it's ghosts of the Spaniards that guard the gold—that the skeletons of the long dead rise up to defend the treasure."

"But that's nonsense!" Sarah protested.

"Yeah, but the point is, there are a lot of wild stories about things in those mountains. You can't believe everything you hear."

"I know," Sarah agreed with a troubled frown. "Timothy didn't believe the story at first, either. But when he checked into it, he actually found the names of the men who were in the expedition. He traced the family of one of them who had been killed in the war. The man's son lived in Virginia, and Timothy went and talked to him. The son remembered his father telling about the expedition, and from him Timothy learned that one of the treasure hunters is still alive."

Despite himself, Stark found his interest growing. "Alive? After this long?"

Sarah gave a quick emphatic nod. "Yes, his name is Wills Bannister. He was eighteen when he joined the expedition—just a boy. Timothy located him and came here to Oklahoma Territory to visit him. Afterward Timothy came home almost frantic with excitement. Bannister identified the silk map as the original of the one the expedition used. Timothy arranged for a leave of absence from the university and returned here so he and Bannister could go into the Wichitas in search of the gold. The last letter I had from him said they were ready to leave." For the first time her voice faltered.

"How long ago was that?" Prudence asked gently.

Sarah swallowed hard. "Over six months ago." Her eyes were suddenly full of moisture, which she blinked stubbornly away.

"And you haven't heard from him since?" Stark prodded.

Wordlessly she shook her head, and Prudence rose to slip a comforting arm around her shoulders. Stark looked out over the pastureland and sipped his lemonade, giving the girl a moment to regain her composure.

"Where did this Wills Bannister live?" he asked finally.

"White City."

A low whistle escaped Stark's lips. "Your fiance went there and came back? That's a miracle in itself."

"Why? What do you know about White City?"

"It's a tough place," Stark answered. "Nowadays they call it Beer City. It's northwest of here, up near Liberal, Kansas. It's located in the Public Land Strip between Oklahoma Territory and the Kansas border, where no laws apply. The whole place is nothing but a sinkhole of corruption spawned to serve the cowboys and cattlemen driving their herds to the railhead. It's mostly a collection of bawdy houses and saloons patronized by the scum of the earth—thieves, murderers, gunmen, gamblers. I doubt there's anyone there who could even remotely be called a reputable citizen."

Sarah shuddered. "Then you think this Wills Bannister might have somehow betrayed Timothy?"

He shrugged. "It's possible. Do you know for certain they left White City?"

Some of her assurance returned. "They went to

Liberal to purchase supplies. I managed to learn that by sending telegrams of inquiry to the law enforcement officials of all the towns I thought they might have possibly passed through."

She was thorough and resourceful, Stark admitted to himself, and not without intelligence. "Why did you come to see me?" he asked flatly.

"I want to hire you to go into the Wichitas with me to look for Timothy."

Stark leaned back in his chair and observed her for a long time. "There's more you're not telling me," he said at last.

She appeared almost relieved at his words. "When Timothy was researching the legend about the treasure, he came into contact somehow with a—a fortune hunter, I guess you'd call him. A man named Douglas Brockton. Timothy thought at first Brockton might know something about the actual location of the Cave with the Iron Door. But he finally realized Brockton was just leading him on in hopes of eventually getting the treasure himself."

Sarah went on to say Timothy had done his best to sever ties with Brockton. However, after Timothy left for White City, Brockton had reappeared and tried to learn Timothy's whereabouts from her.

"Then abruptly Brockton quit contacting me," she said with a touch of fear in her voice. "Initially I was relieved. I thought he'd given up. But when I hired a detective from New York to go to White City to locate Timothy, the man returned with news of Brockton's presence in the town along with a number of hired gunmen. After making his report, the detective quit with no explanation. I think Brockton or his gunmen must have scared him off."

"But why would Brockton stay in White City if

Timothy has already left for the Wichitas?" Prudence asked in puzzlement. "Why wouldn't he just follow him on his quest?"

"Timothy's exceptionally intelligent," Sarah said with a note of pride in her voice. "I think he must've given Brockton the slip. But he left a copy of the map hidden in White City. He wanted to make sure there was a way to trace him if he disappeared. He notified me of what he'd done, and somehow Brockton might've gotten word of that hidden map."

"Except he doesn't know where the map is," Stark finished for her, "and you do."

She nodded and seemed about to add something, but held back. Stark's gaze on her was steady. He sensed she wanted him to know everything, but at the same time was reluctant to tell him for fear of scaring him off. She was playing games, and it wasn't easy for her. He felt a curious mix of sympathy and irritation.

"Well, it's not hard to figure out Brockton got word you were coming out here and sent those four gunmen after you this afternoon. He thinks if he has hold of you he can force you to disclose where the map is hidden."

Again she looked relieved that he'd guessed the reason for her reluctance. "That's right. And you got a glimpse of the tactics he uses this afternoon. Are you willing to help me find Timothy knowing the risk involved?"

Stark glanced at Prudence. She wore a pensive frown. This was the first she'd heard of the confrontation this afternoon, and he knew she couldn't be too happy about it. She'd rested a lot easier since he'd turned his interest more toward raising horses. She wouldn't take too kindly to him hiring on for a job so fraught with danger—and senseless danger to boot.

A search for a lost gold mine. How futile was that?

Stark decided to take a minute before answering. "How did you find me?" he stalled.

She wet her lips. "That first detective I engaged suggested I contact you if I decided to come to the territory. He said he'd worked on a case with you several years ago when you were with the Pinkertons." She leaned forward slightly as if seeking to impel him by the sheer force of her will. "Please go with me. I can pay your usual fees."

Stark sensed the girl's strength, her resolve, and remembered the four men on the trail. Brockton, whoever he was, played rough. Stark realized that if he turned Sarah down, she would only try to find someone else to guide her. And failing that, she would go on by herself. But all her grit and determination would carry no weight against Brockton and the savage men he employed. She would have no chance, would be as helpless as a newborn colt against a pack of timber wolves.

"I'll go," he said quietly.

The light of pleasure that flashed in Sarah's eyes was offset by the fear and worry he saw in Prudence's. He didn't look forward to trying to make his wife understand this one.

However, Prudence's tone was pleasant when she spoke. "Sarah, I don't know all that went on this afternoon, but I think it would be safer if you stayed here with us tonight."

"Oh, but I couldn't impose," Sarah insisted quickly. "I've already checked in at a hotel in town."

"We'll send one of the hands for your luggage," Prudence said. "I insist you stay."

Sarah glanced out at the lengthening shadows stealing across the rolling pastures. "Well, I'll have to admit I wasn't looking forward to the ride back to town."

"Then it's settled. Now I'm sure you'll want to freshen up before dinner. We'll eat in about an hour." Prudence turned to Inez, who had appeared to take the pitcher and glasses away. "Inez, will you please show Miss Walker to the guest room."

The housekeeper nodded, and with a grateful smile, Sarah followed the woman inside.

Stark couldn't bring himself to look at his wife. He stared off at the horizon, remembering the rugged harshness of the Wichitas, the feel of the rifle kicking in his hands as he fired at the gunmen this afternoon. He wasn't sure, but he thought the hot summer breeze now carried a faint chill with it.

After a moment, Prudence sank into the chair beside him, and he steeled himself for the sharp words he was sure would follow. Instead she reached out and took his hand. He looked over at her, surprised to see a tender look glowing in her dark eyes.

He couldn't keep the puzzlement out of his voice. "I thought you'd be upset I took this job," he ventured.

"On one level I am," she said evenly. "But on another I'm glad you agreed to go with her."

He shook his head in bewilderment. "You're gonna have to explain this one to me, love, 'cause right now I don't have a clue."

"It's easy." Prudence's eyes misted. "She loves that boy, Jim, in the deepest and truest sense of the word. If she can't find anyone to go with her, she'll go on alone."

"I could tell that. I just didn't realize you could."

"Oh, it's obvious. I couldn't miss it." She leaned toward him. "And since she's set on going, I'm glad she'll have you on her side."

He stretched across and gave her a quick kiss. "I'll never figure you out, Mrs. Stark. You amaze me more each day. This trek is liable to take a while, though, and I'm sure gonna miss you."

"No, you won't," Prudence said flatly. "I'm going with you."

Stark stiffened in his chair and opened his mouth to protest, but then thought better of it. "Any use in me trotting out the usual reasons why it's not a good idea for you to go along?"

"Nope." She shook her head for emphasis. "You might as well save your breath. My mind's made up."

Stark sighed. In all the years he'd known her—even before they were married—she'd had the infuriating habit of dealing herself into his cases. She was an intelligent woman with the connections and resources to get her way with or without his help or permission. He'd just gradually come to accept that it was better for him to let her in from the start. At least that way he had her close and he could keep an eye out for her safety.

And vice versa.

More than once she'd saved his bacon. He'd be hard pressed to find anyone he'd rather have siding him in a pinch. Considering the perilous undertones of this mission, he almost felt relieved to have such a trusted ally along.

Chapter Three

It was well after midnight, and Prudence couldn't sleep. She rose quietly without waking Jim, who was slumbering peacefully beside her.

Before he fell asleep, he'd told her about the events of the afternoon—of his rescue of Sarah from the four gunmen. She could picture the scene all too vividly in her mind, and that picture was keeping slumber at bay. She slipped into her robe and silently left their bedroom.

The evening was still hot, and she hoped some fresh air would help calm the restlessness she felt. She descended the stairs and stepped out onto the broad front porch. She was surprised to find Sarah Walker already there. The girl spun around, the fright obvious on her face in the bright moonlight.

"I'm sorry I startled you," Prudence apologized in a low voice. "I couldn't sleep and thought some air might help."

"Yeah, me too." Sarah laughed shakily. "I really haven't had a good night's sleep since I left New York City. I think it's all this peace and quiet."

Prudence smiled in spite of herself at the girl's effort

25

to lighten the mood. "Yes, this must be entirely different than the world you're used to."

"That's an understatement," Sarah said with another nervous laugh. "I really admire you. You seem so at home and comfortable in this frontier environment. I don't think I have the type of personality to be able to live out here. It must require a lot of courage, and I'm not very brave."

"You've got to be kidding," Prudence reprimanded mildly. "Surely you realize it took a lot of courage to come out here looking for your fiance."

"But I had no choice," Sarah protested. "I had to come. I might be the only hope Timothy has of rescue. It was an act of total desperation on my part, and I've been practically quaking with fear every step of the way."

"That's what courage is all about—acting in spite of fear. It takes no courage at all to do things you're comfortable with and act in situations where there's no danger."

Sarah looked thoughtful. "I never looked at it like that. I've just always felt like such a coward."

"Well, you're not. In fact, I would think you'd feel out of place in a 'staid, settled' environment. You obviously have a very strong will and a mind of your own— not very sought after qualities in a 'lady,' if I remember Eastern gentility correctly."

Sarah's smile was genuine this time. "Well, actually I do chafe a bit under restrictions. Timothy and I both have fine minds, and we share an insatiable curiosity and thirst for knowledge. Yet he was allowed to go to the university, and my family never gave me that option. It seems to me that women should be given an equal chance to pursue their dreams and develop their abilities. Regretfully, that isn't so."

"Still, things are changing gradually," Prudence said quietly.

"Yes, of course they are." Sarah sounded somewhat embarrassed. "You're living proof of that, aren't you? You must be very proud of what you've accomplished. I'm sure you had a lot of social and professional barriers to overcome. It must have been quite a struggle."

"Not as much of a struggle as you might think. Unlike you, I had the full support of my father, and that made all the difference in the world. Is there any way you could make your family see how important an education is to you?"

"No, I'm afraid it's too late for that. My parents both died a few years back from influenza. Timothy understands, however. As soon as we're married, he wants me to begin taking some courses at the university. We've known each other since childhood, and he's been a wonderful comfort to me through many trials. I couldn't have made it after my parents' death without him." She lowered her eyes. "That's why it's so important that I find him. He's really all I have left."

Prudence felt an overwhelming surge of sympathy for the girl. "Don't worry. Jim will help you find Timothy if he's—" The rest of the sentence died unspoken. Prudence couldn't believe she'd been so thoughtless.

"If he's still alive?" Sarah finished for her.

Prudence reached out and caught the girl's hand. "I'm so sorry. That just slipped out. I didn't intend to be cruel."

Sarah looked at her with tears glistening on her cheeks. "Don't worry about it. I've had that thought dozens of times."

"Of course you have," Prudence said comfortingly. "You're a bright girl, and you can see the danger. You even experienced it first hand today."

"Yes, that encounter was sobering," Sarah admitted, wiping the tears away with the back of her hand. "You can't be too happy about your husband taking on a job like this when you've just begun to build your life together. I understand how you must feel. Why don't I look for someone else to accompany me? Perhaps Mr. Stark could recommend someone . . ."

"There is no one else!" The sharpness of Prudence's words startled even her. "Look, I told you that you had courage, and I meant it. But don't let that go to your head. You're a greenhorn in a basically hostile land. You've already beaten the odds by making it this far in one piece."

Sarah appeared visibly shaken by the statement, but Prudence couldn't bring herself to soften the impact. Not one particle of her being doubted the truth of her words, and the girl needed to realize the gravity of the situation.

"As much as I hate to say this," she continued, "Jim is the only one in this area, maybe even in the whole territory, who stands a chance of getting you in and out of those mountains alive."

Sarah stared at her with a shocked look on her face. There was a quiver of fear in her voice when she finally spoke. "But why are you concerned with my problems? You never even laid eyes on me before yesterday. Why should you care if I make it back safely?"

The girl's question crystallized the war of emotions vying for prominence inside her, Prudence realized. Selfishly, she hated to think of Jim going up against such overwhelming odds. But at the same time, just as she had said, there was no one else who could do the job successfully. With that degree of competence came responsibility—a responsibility that Jim took very seriously.

And now that she was married to him, it was a responsibility that she must share.

"Because . . . because you love Timothy the same way I love Jim. And if Jim were missing, I would set out to find him. And I would hope that people along the way would care enough to help me. It's a simple matter of human decency."

Stark glimpsed the familiar bearded face on the boardwalk across the busy street as he swung down from Red. Reflexively his hand jumped toward the Colt Peacemaker revolver holstered at his side even as his feet hit the ground.

Red stood steady, but the bay gelding on the short lead shied at his unexpected movement and for a moment, Stark's view was blocked. He stepped fast sideways, eyes searching the confusion of horsemen, pedestrians and wagons. But the face was gone. Vanished. Still he had no doubt that he had just seen the bearded leader of the owlhoots who had accosted Sarah the day before at his ranch.

He headed across the street, leaving Red unhitched. The stud, he knew, would wait for him. And the pack-horse tethered to the saddle horn wouldn't be going anywhere on his own.

Stark dodged between a rider and a wagon coming from opposite directions and made it to the far board-walk. The mouth of an alley opened before him, running between a frame saloon and another building. Still no sign of his quarry, and Stark felt a scowl pull at his features. If he could catch the man he might be able to learn for sure why they had been after Sarah, and if it was, indeed, the enigmatic Douglas Brockton who had hired him and his cronies. At any rate, it was worth an effort.

He moved close to the wall as he entered the alley. It was narrow, filled with refuse dropped from the windows of the saloon's second floor. He palmed the revolver and moved swiftly forward. At the end of the alley a wooden door opened into the building housing the saloon. It stood slightly ajar.

The saloon was a natural refuge for vermin such as he was pursuing. Cautiously he shoved the door open, dropping to one knee before he did so, barrel of the revolver probing into the gloom. He found himself looking into a small foyer area. Rickety stairs led both up and down. Another door leading presumably to the public area of the saloon was to his right. He hesitated only briefly. Instinct told him the man had fled to the lower level. A rat would always go to ground.

The wooden stairs led down into dank gloom, shifting unnervingly beneath his weight. Stark guessed he was descending into a section of the tunnel system underlying parts of Guthrie.

In addition to providing protected passage between various reputable establishments in town, parts of the elaborate tunnel system also served to permit clandestine access to the lairs of the more unsavory denizens of the city.

Stark had used the tunnel system himself at times on various errands, but he was not familiar with all of it. He wondered if anyone really was. Certainly, the thought came, there was a good chance his prey was far more at home in this portion than he was.

He froze as he detected a sound below him. A booted foot on packed earth? He had pulled the outside door shut behind him so as not to be silhouetted in its light, and his eyes had not yet become accustomed to the dimness. Was the bearded man even now waiting there below for him to descend?

He eased down another step, then another, trying to step lightly, to settle his weight gradually upon each tread. Even if his prey waited in ambush, he told himself the fellow could not be able to see much better than he.

Another step and he could discern the foot of the stairs. He paused to listen again, and this time he was certain he heard receding footsteps. The passageway seemed to take a square turn at the bottom of the stairway, and now he could detect a faint glow of a lantern or oil lamp suspended part way down the tunnel.

He took the last four steps in two strides and ducked fast around the corner. He found himself in a fifty-foot stretch of earthen corridor buttressed by timbers at infrequent intervals. A single lantern swung from one such buttress midway down the corridor. At the far end a shadowy figure dodged from sight around another turn. Stark's pistol came up, but there wasn't time for a measured shot. He didn't really want to risk killing the man, only to apprehend him for a few questions.

The light of the swinging lantern cast grotesque shadows as he rushed forward. His quarry must have brushed it in passing, Stark guessed. The bearded man was a fool not to have extinguished it, but then men of his ilk were rarely long on brains. Stark paused to lift the lantern chimney and blow out the flame. Now his own distorted shadow would not precede him up the passage.

A dim illumination came from around the corner up ahead. He drew up as he reached it. His prey had shown no inclination to turn and fight, but still only a greenhorn took a fool's chance. In a single smooth motion he ducked around the corner and dropped to one knee.

The roaring muzzle flame stabbed at him out of the gloom ahead. He actually heard the slug glance from the earthen wall beside his head as dirt exploded into his eyes. He fell sidewise, triggering blindly at the figure he had glimpsed on the stairs in front of him. Another shot blasted in return, the slug whipcracking over his head. Desperately he scrambled back around the corner, rubbing at his stinging blinded eyes.

Dimly, even over the slamming echoes, he heard the pounding of footsteps on the wooden stairway, the slam of the closing door. He came to his knees, knuckling his eyes, the gun still clenched in his right fist. Just as a rat would go to ground, so also could it turn savagely upon its pursuer.

He made it to his feet and retreated a few steps, keeping the revolver leveled in the direction of the corner. He was sure the bearded man had fled following his abortive ambush, but there was no point in playing the amateur.

His vision was beginning to return, though blurred by tears. That first shot had only missed him by inches. By the grace of God, he amended reverently.

He edged back to the corner and peered around it. By the faint light of another lantern at the far end of the tunnel he could make out the ramshackle stairway where his ambusher had stood. It was empty now, as was the small landing at its top when he reached it. Making a cautious exit through the trap door, he found himself in a deserted rundown barn that must have once served as a stable. He wondered what nefarious practices had led to the construction of this part of the tunnel in years past.

There was no sign of the bearded hardcase. The way the man had fled and fought to avoid capture more or less confirmed Stark's suspicion that he had been left behind to keep track of the expedition's progress. The outlaw had probably been watching the spread since

Sarah had taken up residence with him and Prudence the night before. Stark only wished he'd had the chance to question the hombre as to the particulars of his assignment.

The old barn fronted an unpaved sidestreet, and he dusted himself off and replaced the spent shell in his revolver before stepping out into the sunlight.

Time to get the law's take on the situation.

Deputy U.S. Marshall Evett Nix was just emerging from the door to his cellblock as Stark entered the office. He grinned now as he motioned Stark into a chair facing his desk. Over the years the two men had developed a rough camaraderie of two pros traveling toward the same goal by different roads. They'd both snagged their share of outlaws. Nix just had to work within a few more constraints than Stark did.

Briefly, Stark explained his alliance with Sarah and described the encounter with the gunmen on his land and his fruitless effort to apprehend one of them today. "The girl thinks her fiance, this Timothy Rankin, might be in some kind of trouble. And it's likely an Eastern shyster named Douglas Brockton is behind it."

Nix leaned his chair back against the wall. "What's this Brockton look like?"

"Sarah says he's tall, handsome, and dresses like a lawyer. She insists he even talks like one."

"Well, of course we got lots of lawyer types around here," Nix allowed with a smirk, "but no strangers from back East that I've noticed. I'll keep my eyes open for him, though, and for the other ones you described. Where was this Timothy Rankin last seen? Maybe I can wire the law thereabouts and get a lead on him."

It was Stark's turn to smirk. "White City."

The Marshall came erect in his chair. "Beer City? You crazy taking a woman up there?"

Stark sighed. "Two women. Prudence insists on going too."

Nix shook his head. "I might've figured as much. Still, Prudence isn't the greenhorn this New York girl is. Your wife can at least sit a horse and shoot a gun."

"The girl's a passable horsewoman herself," Stark opined. "She managed to outrun four gunmen for a respectable distance yesterday."

"I suppose that is to her credit," Nix agreed. "But I suggest you get her a gun and teach her to use it."

"I already thought of that. She's waiting with Prudence over at the office. I dropped them off right before I encountered the bearded outlaw. I need to have the packhorse reshod, then I'm gonna take Sarah gun shopping while Prudence clears her calendar for the trip. We'll probably leave out early in the morning."

"Well, good luck. I don't guess I'm going to be of much help in this escapade. Forget me contacting the local law for you. Up where you're going, there ain't any. That's outside my jurisdiction. But, of course, you know that."

"Yeah," Stark said dryly. "I know it all too well."

A few hours later Stark stopped with Sarah in front of a low brick structure with an inscription on the door that read, RAMIREZ AND SONS, GUNSMITHS. Inside, handguns were displayed in the glass case, and an assortment of rifles decorated the walls. Various apparatuses for working on guns, including a cartridge loading setup were visible in the back part of the shop.

As they entered, Luis Ramirez himself turned away from poring over a six-gun held in a vice. His dark weathered face lit up as he saw Stark. "Ah, my amigo, and a beautiful young senorita. What can I do for you?"

Stark gripped the older man's callused hand warmly.

"The lady needs a gun. Actually, a handgun and a rifle." He turned to the girl. "Have you ever shot a gun before?"

Sarah regarded him levelly. "We went to the hunt club sometimes at home. I've fired rifles and shotguns."

"That is good." Ramirez came forward and reached out to take her right hand in both of his. He held it for a moment, squeezing it, flexing it. "Ah, strong hands. A horsewoman, I would bet."

Sarah nodded confirmation, obviously pleased.

Ramirez released her hand and retreated behind the counter. The Mexican was short and muscular, all wiry sinew and bone. Despite the gray in his dark hair, he moved with quick agility. He glanced over his selection, then with an emphatic nod produced a small revolver with a short barrel. "Here. Small caliber for a lady, but seven shots instead of six to make up for it."

He handed the firearm to Stark, who examined it closely, checking to be sure it was unloaded. "What make is this?" he asked.

Luis grinned proudly. "It is a Ramirez. My sons and I hope to produce many more. I myself have tested it, and I personally guarantee that it is accurate and reliable."

"It's a real nice piece," Stark affirmed. "Thirty-two caliber, I see." He passed the gun to Sarah, who took it carefully. He was pleased to note that she kept the barrel pointed safely downward.

"You're sure you can teach me to use this properly?" she asked skeptically. "I never thought of wearing a sidearm."

Stark chuckled. "If I can teach my wife to shoot, I can teach anyone."

Ramirez erupted in a hearty laugh that made Sarah eye them both suspiciously.

Stark's face dissolved into a rare smile. "I'm not

making fun of Prudence," he explained warmly. "It's just that she was totally against all forms of 'force and violence' when we met. Since then she's come to see that sometimes it's necessary. She's changed me a lot over the years as well. Why, before I met her, nobody in this territory would've ever picked me to become an old married horse rancher. Right, Luis?"

"How right you are, senor." Ramirez agreed with another laugh.

For a rifle they settled on a Winchester repeater, identical to the one Prudence carried. Sarah hefted it with an easy competence that was reassuring to Stark. At least now they'd have another gun to oppose Brockton and whatever other dangers awaited them. But that was still long odds, he reflected.

"Luis," he said suddenly, "what do you know of the Lost Cave with the Iron Door?"

Ramirez froze in the act of placing boxes of shells on the counter. His dark eyes clouded with concern. "It is a myth. A tale for children. My people have spoken of it for years."

"What if it is real?" Sarah asked quietly.

Scorn crept into his voice. "Real or not, it is the work of the devil. No one has ever found it, and the bones of those who have tried litter the Wichita Mountains."

Stark studied Sarah for a moment and saw that the Mexican's warning had done nothing to dampen her fervor for the dangerous trek. If anything, the cold light of purpose in her eyes glittered even brighter. It spoke well of her love for her fiance perhaps, but not so well of good sense and sound judgment.

He felt a new surge of unease. It had been a long time since he'd felt such an intense foreboding about a mission.

Chapter Four

They left at daybreak the next morning. Stark led out with the packhorse in tow. Prudence and Sarah rode side by side behind him. They rode in silence as they skirted the edge of Guthrie. The only sound in the post-dawn quiet was the gentle clopping of the horses' hooves on the packed earth.

The air was clean and cool, not yet warmed by the sun which was only moments above the horizon. As they hit the well-traveled road that led westward across the rolling grasslands, Prudence glanced over at Sarah. "Excited?" she asked.

The girl nodded. "It's been so long since I've heard from Timothy. It's good to finally be doing something definite to locate him. I just hope it's not too late."

Prudence caught the note of apprehension in Sarah's voice and again regretted thoughtlessly planting the idea that harm might have befallen Timothy.

"He's been gone so long," Sarah continued, "that it's becoming a real struggle to make ends meet financially."

"How have you been living?"

"My parents left a small estate. Of course, it's pretty depleted now. When I return I'll probably have to sell my house. It's quite close to the campus, and Timothy and I planned to live there after we were married. But if he's gone . . ."

"Sarah, let's not visit that possibility just yet," Prudence said firmly. "You traveled here to Oklahoma Territory believing Timothy was alive, and nothing has happened since your arrival to prove otherwise."

"That's not entirely true," Sarah admitted shakily. "I came to find out *whether or not* he's alive. It's the not knowing that's so hard." She looked over at Prudence with tears in her eyes. "Oh, don't get me wrong. I want desperately for him to be all right. We've planned our whole life together, and it's a wonderful life. My world will become a nightmare without him."

Prudence knew the girl was upset, but she couldn't help but feel Sarah was exaggerating somewhat. "No matter what happens, I'm sure things will work out fine for you," she offered reassuringly.

"But you don't understand," Sarah persisted. "A woman in my precarious financial position has very few options—the most widely accepted and least appealing would be entering a 'suitable marriage' to a man who could 'provide for me.' I don't want that."

"Of course you don't. Nobody would. And what makes you think I wouldn't understand?"

"Because you've always been in control of your destiny," Sarah returned. "It's quite different for me. I've more or less been forced to live as the men in my life decreed."

Prudence shifted slightly in the saddle and fixed her with a direct gaze. "So, if you could have it your way, what would you want out of life?"

Confusion was evident in Sarah's eyes. "I don't

know exactly—perhaps I just want a chance to explore and discover for myself what would make me happy. Timothy wanted desperately to give me that chance. Any other man would just think it was silly. I suspect that's why finding the gold was so important to him. When he was packing for this trip he kept going on and on about how the money would allow us to travel and how I could finally take the classes I wanted at the university . . ."

Prudence didn't quite know what to say. There were certainly no easy answers in this situation.

"It's funny now, though," Sarah continued. "I wish I'd told him all that wasn't important to me. I wish I had urged him to stay in New York City with me. I don't really care about the gold, about being rich. I only care about having him back safe and sound."

For the first time since the conversation began, Stark turned around in the saddle to offer a comment. "If this is the tone the conversation's going to take for the rest of the trip, I vote we turn around and go home."

Sarah looked up startled. "I-I didn't mean to sound negative. I guess I felt like I needed to finally face reality."

"The only reality we're facing right now is trying to put ourselves a lotta miles closer to White City by sundown. There's a verse in the Bible that says each day's troubles are sufficient thereof. I think that's the good Lord's way of telling us to take each day as it comes."

"Of course you're right, Mr. Stark." Sarah was obviously forcing a more positive tone into her voice. "I'll try harder to remain optimistic."

"I figure there's one thing for sure on our side," Stark continued. "If Brockton had Timothy, he wouldn't be hounding you so hard. To me that says that at least the crooks think your fiance is alive."

Prudence didn't quite understand Jim's logic in making the statement. However, it did serve to restore the spark of hope in Sarah's eyes which her own careless words had extinguished the night before. For that she was grateful.

The miles melted away as the temperature rose steadily with the sun. By midmorning Prudence's clothes felt sticky and damp with perspiration. As they rode on, the homesteads gradually became farther apart and less prosperous, and the road became no more than a rutted track that stretched away across endless miles of rolling grasslands.

The tall two-story farmhouses immediately surrounding Guthrie gave way to squat one-story gray shanties and rough-hewn log cabins. Then, as the trees became more scarce on the prairie, odd flat-roofed huts made from primitively shaped blocks of clay began to appear.

Noticing Sarah's curious stare as they passed practically through the dooryard of one such farm, Prudence nodded toward the house and said, "They call that a 'soddy.' "

Sarah returned the waves of several dirty-faced barefoot children who ceased playing to watch their passage. "What in the world is it made of?"

"Blocks of sod stacked row upon row."

"I must say that seems an unorthodox building material."

Prudence couldn't help smiling. "Not really. Considering the circumstances, it's pretty ingenious. I suppose you've noticed the lack of trees. There was no lumber to build cabins, so the settlers used the materials at hand."

"But isn't it difficult to cut the soil into blocks?"

"No, in fact the blocks of soil are a byproduct of the

farming methods. The buffalo grass is so deep-rooted and thick it has to be cut away with a special plow to open the fields for planting. The plows turn the sod upside down in long slabs. The farmers then take the slabs and stack them to form the walls of their cabins."

Sarah looked back at the soddy with new respect. "It's remarkable that those people have made use of such materials."

"They had no choice," Stark said over his shoulder. "They had to use what was available or pull up stakes and head back where they came from."

Sarah smiled sheepishly over at Prudence. "See, that's what I mean by courage. I don't think I could live like that."

"Sure you could, if you had to." Prudence couldn't resist teasing the girl a little. "That's not the worst of it. They use cow manure for heating fuel."

Sarah shuddered. "You made that up."

"She's telling the gospel truth," Stark called back. "Why, a bucket of dried cow chips kindled with grass makes a good bed of cooking coals. I've used it myself many times out on the trail."

"It sounds utterly disgusting."

"Nevertheless," Prudence continued, "it's an efficient cheap fuel. So much is used, in fact, that a lot of homesteaders make yearly trips into Texas to the big cattle ranches on cow chip gathering expeditions."

"Yep," Stark added, "mom, pop, and all the kids take washtubs and drag them behind them until they're full, then dump them into their wagon. Why, I heard a farmer brag one time that he and his family had a fuel pile bigger than their cabin."

Prudence was glad Jim was in a talkative mood. He continued to regale Sarah with stories about the rigors of pioneer life as the sun climbed higher in the sky. All in all it was a pleasant diversion that kept the girl from dwelling on the probable fate of her beloved Timothy.

At noon they stopped to eat under a lonely stand of cottonwoods beside a small stream. Prudence left Sarah to break out the rations while she followed Stark down to the stream to water the horses.

"Thanks for finding a way to encourage Sarah about Timothy," she ventured. "I hope your reasoning is correct."

"Oh, it's correct, all right. If Brockton had gotten hold of Timothy, he and his gang of cutthroats would be on their way to the Wichitas by now."

"Not necessarily," Prudence protested. "Maybe they caught Timothy and killed him trying to make him talk."

"Nope. That couldn't happen," Stark said tersely.

Prudence felt a tingle of fear creep up her spine, and dreaded asking the next logical question. "Why not?"

"Because Brockton probably has someone on his payroll who's an expert at making people talk. There are men out there who build a whole reputation on torture for information. A greenhorn like Timothy Rankin would have been spilling his guts by sunset if such a man got hold of him. Brockton would have known all Timothy knew in short order."

"And the same holds true for Sarah," Prudence gasped. "If Brockton had captured her, she would have suffered the same fate."

"Yeah, only worse, since she's a woman."

Prudence refused to let her mind take in all that his words entailed. "So Timothy actually put her in grave danger by telling her where the copy of the map is hidden."

Stark nodded curtly.

"Oh, Jim," Prudence cried in an urgent whisper.

"Maybe we should just be honest with her and try to get her to turn back."

"I think we both know that wouldn't work," Stark said flatly. "And I'm not sure she'd even be safe if we convinced her to head back to New York. Brockton could take her off a train or grab her out of a hotel somewhere between here and there, and no one would ever be the wiser. You said she has no family, right?"

Prudence shook her head mutely.

Stark's expression remained grim. "So the safest place for her is right here with us, as hard as that might be to accept."

Prudence felt the weight of responsibility settle even heavier upon her shoulders. Her assertion of the night before rang in her mind with frightening clarity. Except now she realized her claim hadn't been broad enough. Not only was Jim the one person who could get Sarah in and out of the Wichita Mountains alive, he was also the one person who could keep her alive—period.

The awareness of it tingled in Stark's blood, danced along his nerves, raised the hairs at the nape of his neck. He shifted in the saddle, eyes scanning the slightly rolling grassland over which they had passed. Instinctively, barely realizing he was doing it, he loosened the shotgun in its sheath.

"What's wrong?" Prudence slowed her mare and divided her attention between him and their backtrail.

Stark didn't look at her. "We're being followed."

Sarah's head swung sharply around, the movement making her blond hair gleam in the afternoon sunlight. "Have you seen them?"

"No. But I think we picked them up when we broke camp this morning. They probably caught up with us overnight."

"But if you haven't seen them, how do you know?"
Stark bristled at her challenge. "I just know."

"It's instinct," Prudence said to soothe the tension.
"Jim has a certain sixth sense about these things."

The girl moistened her lips nervously. "Brockton's
men?"

"I wouldn't bet against it," Stark answered.

Of course, he added to himself, their stalkers could
well be hostile and still not prove to be Brockton's men.
As they neared White City, they penetrated ever deeper into the no man's land of Oklahoma Territory
beyond the protection of Evett Nix and his men.

Long a haven for outlaws and renegades, the area
had become even more dangerous as inexperienced settlers moved in, serving to make the lawless inhabitants
all the more bold and daring as access to easy prey
increased.

He didn't share that thought with the women.

"What do we do now?" Sarah asked anxiously.

"We keep riding for now," he told her. "Don't let on
that we know they're back there. Over the next hill yon-
der, we'll pull up and see if I can spot them."

They jigged their horses forward. The land had flat-
tened some as they moved northwest, but there were
still occasional rolling hills swelling the landscape.
And they were seeing fewer and fewer homesteads now,
further evidence of the prevalence of lawlessness in the
area. About noon they had passed a collapsed storm
cellar beside the start of a log cabin. There was no clue
as to why the structure had been left unfinished on the
lonely prairie.

They crested the hill, and about twenty feet down the
far side, Stark pulled Red to a halt. The women drew up
beside him. Prudence wore a worried frown. He hand-

ed her the packhorse's lead. "You two can get off if you want. I may be a few minutes."

He dismounted and loosened Red's reins, leaving the stud to graze around his bit. He took a pair of binoculars from his saddlebags, and moving in a crouch, headed back up the hill. Near the top, he dropped flat and snaked his way on his belly to the summit where he could view their backtrail without being silhouetted against the skyline.

Using the binoculars, he scanned the terrain. Nothing. Only tall grass, waving slightly in the slow wind. He lowered the field glasses and squinted with naked eyes. Still nothing. He raised the binoculars and repeated the survey.

"I've got 'em," he called down to the women.

Five riders had materialized out of a draw about a mile distant. He pressed the binoculars hard against his face, but the distance was too great to discern details. It didn't matter who they were. Five horsemen riding so determinedly in their wake spelled trouble whether they were Brockton's men or not.

He eased back down the hill and stood up, brushing the grass and dust from his clothes.

"What now?" Sarah asked, the strain evident in her voice.

"We keep moving." Stark swung back aboard Red as the women remounted. "This country's too open for them to try anything in the daylight. But come nightfall, it's a different story. That's when they'll try to take us if they're going to at all. But now that we know they're back there, we can pick the ground and be waiting for them."

Stark stopped twice more before dark to verify that the riders were still behind them. As the sun dropped closer to the horizon, he began to study the terrain with a gauging eye. A shallow creek meandered through the grassland, flanked on either side by a few hundred yards of woodland. For their purposes it was ideal.

They had ridden in silence, Sarah's tension betrayed by her frequent glances behind them and the tightness of her pull on her mare's reins. Prudence was doing her best to appear confident and unperturbed, but the strain was obvious in her as well.

"We need to find a clearing," Stark broke the silence at last. He was careful to leave a plain trail where they entered the woods. It wouldn't do for their pursuers to lose them now.

There was a heavy growth of underbrush for the horses to breast. Skirting the worst of it, Stark and the women were kept busy ducking the low-hanging branches which plucked at them. Some distance into the woods, Stark detected a thinning of the brush to their right and moved in that direction.

They emerged in a small natural clearing about a quarter acre in size. A few large trees were scattered about at intervals. A big red-tailed hawk lifted on laboring pinions from a skeletal dead tree and flapped lazily away over the treetops.

Stark surveyed the area with satisfaction. It was just the arena he'd hoped for. He kept a casual watch as he helped the women set up camp. He instructed them to maintain a normal conversation, knowing their voices would carry. He didn't want their trackers to miss them in the brush. Over a dinner of biscuits and salted ham fried in a skillet, he probed the brush with his senses. He detected nothing, however, and felt a growing sense of success.

The five were out there now of a certainty, he thought. And the man in charge was as good as their subtle trailing had suggested. They would have heard voices, smelled the campfire and food, and rather than risk alerting their prey prematurely, had waited for darkness out of sight of the camp.

Arguably then, that added weight to the thought that they were Brockton's men and were aware of Stark's identity and the threat he could pose to five armed men.

And they would learn even more about that threat before the night was through, he vowed silently.

Darkness gathered fast, the shadows caught and held by the encroaching trees. Sarah's face was pale and drawn in the firelight as he told her and Prudence quietly of his plan. Both women nodded understanding with a stern determination when he finished. Stark recalled the closeness and warmth of other nights with Prudence in their new home. But that was gone now, erased by the prevalence of potential violence and death.

As the fire burned low and the gloom pressed close, Stark found himself straining to hear something out there in the woods, to penetrate the darkness with his gaze. At his nod, they began to assemble their bedrolls. In a matter of minutes, three shapes lay unmoving by the dying fire.

Under cover of darkness, they eased away from the camp and into the concealing undergrowth, leaving dummy bedrolls in place. Studying them now, Stark was satisfied. Even to him, there appeared to be people sleeping there in the camp.

Stark was concealed behind the bole of a thick tree at the clearing's edge. Prudence was off to his right under similar cover, and Sarah was to his left where he had placed her behind a fallen tree. She had her Winchester, and he had earlier shown her how to use the curious seven-shot revolver provided by Martinez.

They were facing back in the direction from which they had come. He had been careful in choosing their positions so as to avoid any possibility of a crossfire.

He held the lever-action shotgun lightly in his hands. Grip it too hard and muscles might cramp at a crucial moment. He remembered other nights, other waits for human prey, and wondered how long it would be.

It turned out the wait was comparatively short.

They were good, but he had already guessed that. He had only the faint rustle of leaves for warning, and then, like shadows, the figures began to appear out of the brush on the far side of the camp. He held his breath and counted. Four . . . five. They were all there, in a semi-circle around the opposite side of the clearing. Their leader, whoever he was, had made at least one mistake by not encircling the whole camp. But after all, to his thinking, he had all the camp's occupants accounted for.

Stark couldn't discern details, although none were really necessary. The faint gleam of the embers off the metal of leveled rifles and drawn handguns told him all he needed to know.

He couldn't wait any longer or they would detect the ruse. He stepped partially out from behind the tree, his own gun steady and level. "Right there, every one of you!" he called out sharply.

They began firing at the sound of his voice, before he even completed the warning, guns swiveling to bear on him, blasting with roaring tongues of flame.

But he had expected that reaction, even planned for it. He wheeled back around the tree, spinning to emerge on its other side, dropping to one knee, the shotgun coming to his shoulder in a single smooth movement.

In a clocktick of time he fired, levered, swung the

barrel and fired again, targeting the dark shapes behind the muzzle flashes exploding toward him.

He saw two figures stagger beneath the impact of his slugs. Then he was moving, spinning back around the tree because only a greenhorn didn't change positions after firing at an opponent at night. He came out of his spin and dropped flat, fired, rolled to the side and fired again, dimly aware of other rifles opening up from his right and left. He'd known he could count on Prudence, but it was good to know Sarah hadn't frozen up under fire.

Three of the attackers were down. Two were still flailing, the third was a motionless black form on the ground. The remaining two men were turning to flee, all thought of exchanging further gunfire forgotten. Stark fired high to hasten their flight, then pumped another two slugs at the feet of the two wounded men who were scrambling for cover. They disappeared into the brush after their comrades, leaving the dark form sprawled motionless beside the last dying embers of the fire.

Stark crouched behind the tree and waited, rifle at ready. His ears rang in the aftermath of the gunfire, but he strained to listen, turning occasionally to check his back.

Faintly, the sounds of men on horseback, riding hard through the brush, filtered back to him. The sounds faded rapidly, and Stark started to relax.

"Stay put and don't answer me," he called softly to the women. Then he began a cautious circuit of the camp, keeping to the cover of the undergrowth. The motionless form by the fire still hadn't moved when Stark had satisfied himself that the other attackers had indeed fled.

"Hold your fire," he called, not wanting Prudence or Sarah to shoot him by mistake when he stepped into the open.

He approached the sprawled gunman with care, but there was no need. The man was dead, drilled neatly through the heart by one of Stark's first shots. As he rolled the outlaw over, he saw the bearded man he'd chased through the tunnels of Guthrie. So he'd been right to guess that the man was watching Sarah. He and his cronies must have been trailing them since they'd started.

"Is he dead?"

Stark looked up from where he knelt by the body. Sarah, rifle gripped tightly in her hands, face drawn almost gaunt by the strain, had emerged from concealment and was standing awkwardly a few feet away.

"Yeah, I got him with one of my first shots."

Prudence appeared out of the shadows to slip a comforting arm around the girl's shoulders.

"What about the others?" Sarah persisted in a hoarse whisper.

"We wounded at least two. I doubt they'll come back, but to play it safe, we better break camp and move. In the morning, I'll come back and bury this one."

They dozed fitfully at their new camp on the other side of the creek, each of them taking a turn at sentry duty. As dawn broke, Stark took the small shovel from one of the packs and headed back to take care of the fallen outlaw.

Prudence was worried about the effects the gunfight had had on Sarah. The girl sat listlessly on her horse as they made their way across the endless sea of waving buffalo grass the next morning.

Once again Jim rode up ahead of them, his eyes

relentlessly scanning their surroundings for signs of danger. Prudence saw Sarah's eyes flick to him often, as if fearing he might spot something amiss, as he had done the day before.

"Are you all right, Sarah?" she asked quietly.

Sarah glanced at her and offered a weak smile. "I suppose. I just can't seem to shake the memories of what happened last night. The reports of the guns, those evil shadows lurking about trying to kill us in our sleep . . ."

Not all of us, Prudence thought to herself. Remembering her conversation with Jim, she was sure the men had every intention of taking Sarah to Brockton alive for unimaginable torture. "You can't dwell on it. They didn't succeed, did they?"

"But they might next time," Sarah said in resignation. "Just because we defeated those men last night, doesn't mean it's over. Even I'm smart enough to know hoodlums like that are a dime a dozen. Brockton will have no trouble scrounging up replacements."

"You're right," Prudence agreed ruefully, "particularly in a place like White City."

"So you think the town is as bad as Mr. Stark said?"

"Every bit as much."

"Then I suppose you also agree I'm risking all our lives in an endeavor that is at best risky and at worst completely foolish?"

"No," Prudence contradicted, noticing Sarah's surprise. "You have no choice but to try and find Timothy."

"Still, even supposing we can find the map in White City, there's no guarantee we can read it well enough to locate the lost mine. And if, against all odds, we do find the Cave with the Iron Door, there's certainly no assurance that will lead us to Timothy."

"True," Prudence agreed, "but again we come back

to having no other choice. It's our only lead to your fiance."

"You don't believe in the gold either, do you?" Sarah asked abruptly.

Prudence chose her words carefully, not wanting to upset the girl further. "I don't actually disbelieve, I guess. But this area has spawned a number of tales of lost treasure and forgotten mines. There's the lost Spanish treasure supposedly hidden in Devil's Canyon, and the gold that the conquistadors left near their old fort at Spanish Fort Bend down on the Red River, and the Frenchmen's gold at Sugar Loaf Peak. My father, a noted judge, even confessed to spending some time searching for that particular treasure as a young man."

"Really?" Sarah asked, perking up somewhat.

Prudence nodded. "Yes, he referred to it as his 'youthful folly.' The legend was that a gang of renegade Frenchmen made a living murdering placer miners at a modest gold strike east of Sante Fe in the early 1800s. Eventually, they decided they'd made enough to retire to New Orleans. They hired a Mexican named Lopat to melt the gold into ingots—five hundred to be exact. Then with Lopat as a guide they set out for New Orleans, which at the time was still a French possession."

"The early 1800s—wasn't that about the time of the Louisiana Purchase?" Sarah interrupted.

"Exactly!" Prudence cried. "Very insightful of you. Anyway, en route they learned that Louisiana had been sold to the United States. Unable to decide where else to go, they eventually quarreled and split up, but not before burying the gold near Sugar Loaf Peak up in No Man's Land, not far from White City. Supposedly they marked the site so they could return for it at a later date."

"But why didn't they just divide up the gold when they separated?" Sarah protested.

Prudence shrugged. "Too heavy for one thing, and my father thought each of them was scared to travel alone with that much gold. Anyway, they buried it near a spring and marked the site with four giant Roman numerals spelled out in stones on the prairie. As usual in these stories, the Frenchmen were all killed in one way or another before they could return. Lopat, the Mexican guide, wrote the tale down in the back of his bible years later."

Stark turned around in his saddle and smiled at them. "In the 1870s three of the markers were actually found. I heard the tale when I wasn't much more than a kid and got kind of obsessed with it for a while."

"You never told me that," Prudence said.

"Yeah, me and your father will have something new to talk about next time we see him. Seems we shared an experience. I spent two months scouring the range for that fourth marker, hardly ate or slept the whole time."

"What happened?" Sarah demanded eagerly.

Prudence heard the tone of his voice change subtly, as if he were trying to convey some deeper significance to the girl.

"Two owlhoots who'd heard I was looking for the gold decided I must know more than I did. They waylaid me and tried to make me talk." He paused briefly and there was no emotion in his voice when he continued. "I killed one of them, ran the other one off. I realized then how crazy it was. They, or someone like them, could kill me for information I didn't even have. Or I could spend the rest of my life searching and never even find the fourth marker—much less the gold, if it ever existed. Whatever truth there was to the tale has undoubtedly been distorted by being told and retold around campfires for decades."

"But the other three markers were real?" Sarah persisted.

"Yep, I saw them myself."

"Well, doesn't that prove something?"

"Only that somebody put them there," he answered shortly. "It doesn't have to mean anything about the gold."

"Well, the treasure behind the iron door is real," the girl asserted defensively. "I know it is. Timothy believed it too. He researched it thoroughly before he set out to find it. He's a scholar. He wouldn't get caught up in a wild goose chase!"

Stark gave a shrug. "Maybe the gold *is* real," he admitted. "But look at what it's cost through the years in suffering and lives lost. Think about what it's cost you and Timothy. Is it worth it?"

Prudence knew Stark must have his reasons for forcing Sarah to think about this aspect of the treasure hunt. She rarely questioned his handling of his clients.

But in this case, she felt his timing left a lot to be desired.

Chapter Five

By reflex Stark let his eyes sweep across the prairie, even turning in his saddle to survey their backtrail. He saw nothing to alarm him now.

High overhead a hawk circled, and he had a sudden image of how they must look to the bird from its elevated view—three lonely figures moving across an endless plain beneath a cloudless sky. He wondered if the hawk could see their destination somewhere ahead of them. They were in the Panhandle now, nearing White City, or Beer City as it had come to be known out of the depths of its depravity.

Glancing over his shoulder, he saw Prudence rise slightly in her stirrups to scan the horizon, repeating his survey almost unconsciously. It was a habit she had picked up over the years from his constant watchfulness. There had been no sign of their attackers from the night before, and Stark guessed they'd have no further trouble—from those four at least.

"We've got company," Stark said abruptly, his hand dropping to the sheathed shotgun. Sarah and Prudence anxiously followed his gaze to the two riders he had spotted on the horizon. The men were headed in their direction at a lope, still several hundred yards distant.

Stark unsheathed the shotgun. There was no point in taking any chances. Prudence quickly followed suit, and after an anxious glance at them Sarah did likewise.

"Should we dismount?" Sarah asked.

Stark shook his head. Whoever was approaching wouldn't be able to draw a bead on them from a fast moving horse. If the men slowed down, that would be the time to be concerned.

But the riders apparently wanted no more contact with strangers than they did—particularly strangers who sat awaiting them with unsheathed rifles. The pair veered wide to avoid them, passing well to their left and continuing on without slowing. Stark watched them until they were all but lost in the distance, then put the shotgun away.

"Were they from White City?" Sarah asked nervously.

"Probably." Stark reached for his canteen and drank deeply before answering. His throat was parched, but the water tasted bitter instead of refreshing. He started Red moving again. "We should reach it ourselves in a couple of hours."

"Do you think Brockton will still be there?" The girl's tone was fearful.

"Unless he's found the map, he'll still be there," Stark said flatly. "His kind doesn't give up where gold is concerned. You can give me directions, and I'll go in alone to get the map."

Sarah looked troubled. "Can't we just sneak in and retrieve it and then leave?"

Stark shook his head, irritated that she didn't trust him enough to tell him where the map was. "We need information. I want to see if anyone around there knows anything about Timothy or the old man he went there to meet, Wills Bannister."

"What about Brockton and his men?" Sarah's eyes were wide. "I told you what that detective said. He was scared of them. I'm certain that's why he quit."

"I've never met Brockton, so he doesn't know what I look like. I didn't shave this morning, and with all this trail dust on me, I'll look like any other drifter passing through looking for a good time. There's a good chance I can pick up some information without anyone in his outfit being the wiser."

"But why take such a risk if White City is as bad as you say?"

"There's no if about it," Stark said shortly. "The only reason it ever existed was to provide the cowboys from the trail drives a place to blow off steam. Since Kansas has strict prohibition laws, it was set up to furnish the men with liquor and women in the Public Land Strip along the Kansas border, which is out of the jurisdiction of either Kansas or Oklahoma authorities. It's just a collection of saloons and bawdy houses, with all the scavengers they attract. Some of the local merchants even advertised in area newspapers saying it's the only town of its kind in the civilized world with absolutely no law."

Prudence seemed to sense that Sarah was getting under his skin. She reached out and touched the girl's arm. "Sarah, you hired Jim to handle this search for Timothy. You're just going to have to quit second guessing his decisions."

"I know." The girl bit her lip. "I'm sorry. I'll do whatever you say."

Stark took a deep breath and forced a reasonable tone back into his voice. "Fine. There's a draw up

ahead where you two can wait while I round up supplies and scout out the town. I should be back by sundown. I'll get the map before I return to camp. That is,
if you trust me enough to tell me where it's hidden."

Sarah lowered her eyes. "Of course I trust you. I
didn't mean to infer that I didn't. Timothy wrote that
it's under the floor of Bannister's dilapidated old cabin
on the northeast corner of town. Hopefully the place
won't be that hard to locate."

Stark rode into White City in the afternoon. To the
inhabitants of the town who watched him come, the set
of his stance, the hawk-like gaze of his eyes, and the
easy familiarity with which the Colt Peacemaker rode
his hip marked him as one of their kind.

A rutted dirt street stretched between a motley collection of gaudy, ramshackle frame structures. The
businesses were about equally divided between
saloons, dance halls, and houses of prostitution—some
of them combining two, or even all three of these func-
tions behind their decaying walls. The town had not
been built with permanence in mind, but rather with
quick, illicit profits as a priority. If it was abandoned
tomorrow, Stark thought, the prairie would reclaim the
site within a few years, leaving no trace it had ever
existed.

A trail drive must have recently hit Liberal, Kansas,
with the cowhands coming here to White City for enter-
tainment. The town was an anthill of activity.

He had to move Red aside to make way for a wag-
onload of immodestly clad women, their faces caked
with heavy makeup that bespoke their profession as
blatantly as their attire. They were prostitutes, coming
or going from Liberal, on the hack that made regular
runs between the places. Many of the girls lived in

Liberal and commuted to their decadent marketplace
here in the Public Land Strip. During peak cattle ship-
ping season, ladies of ill repute traveled in from as far
away as Dodge City and Wichita to work their trade in
White City. The sleazy driver of the hack cursed at
Stark as he passed.

Cowboys and drovers lounged in front of saloons or
staggered drunkenly in the company of prostitutes.
Stark rode past the infamous Yellow Snake Saloon.
Pussy Cat Nell, the madam in charge of the house
above the saloon, had once put a load of buckshot in the
would-be town marshal, himself an active cattle rustler.

A crowd had congregated around a raised platform
further down the street. As he drew near, Stark saw two
men stripped to the waist facing one another with
upraised fists. A prizefight—a common event spon-
sored by area merchants to entertain the masses.

Like the Roman circus of old, Stark reflected as he
viewed the two combatants. One of them was plainly
nothing but a cowhand who, through hope of a cash
prize or pressure of his peers, had been persuaded to
climb into the ring against an opponent who was clearly a professional. The latter, a massive blond-haired
man with a heavily muscled physique, stood poised
now before his tottering foe.

The cowhand was clearly on his last legs, his fighting stance a sorry caricature. His face showed the
marks of a brutal beating. Obviously the blond fighter
had not been in any hurry to end the fight. The crowd
pressed close to the elevated ring, jeers and catcalls
sounding from its members. Stark couldn't tell at
which of the fighters they were directed.

As he urged Red wide to skirt the crowd, he saw the
blond grin coldly and go in for the kill, delivering a
savage series of lefts and rights that spun and battered

the hapless cowhand, and ultimately held him upright by their sheer force and number. When the blond stepped back the cowhand collapsed on his face. The crowd cheered mindlessly, and the fighter's manager appeared in the ring to tout the victor. Stark passed on by. The manager's strident voice, calling an offer to all takers, followed him down the street.

He had gone into Liberal alone to restock their supplies, figuring Brockton would be looking for a man traveling with two women. As it was, he had merely appeared to be a lone traveler on a long trek. He had then returned to their campsite and left the packhorse with Prudence and Sarah. They'd set up camp in a wooded draw over a mile outside of town and well hidden from the usual trails. He had extracted a promise from Prudence not to leave the draw until he returned, barring dire emergencies.

Unexpectedly she had hugged him, and he could tell by the turmoil in her eyes that she hated to see him go. He'd dreaded the trip almost as much as she did, but to his way of thinking, it couldn't be avoided. Memories of that look in her eyes stayed with him as he navigated the main street of White City.

With the prizefight behind him, he pulled Red in at The Elephant Saloon and glanced up at the crudely drawn elephant adorning the building. He hesitated before swinging down from the horse. The town, with its pagan decadence, depressed him. He had to resist the sudden urge to turn around and ride out—back to the campsite and the beloved wife who awaited him there.

But in the end the years of cold hard conditioning prevailed. He couldn't pass up the chance to pick up some information about the fate of Timothy Rankin.

The air inside the saloon was stale and hot. The

odors of sweat, whiskey, and tobacco assailed Stark's nostrils as he entered and pushed his way through the close-packed bodies to the bar. Bar girls in low-cut dresses circulated among the patrons, luring them from the bar to the gaming tables in back or to the rooms upstairs with their sagging beds.

A burly bartender took Stark's order for whiskey with a gauging look. Stark put his back to the bar as his eyes swept over the saloon and its inhabitants. No one appeared to be paying him any particular attention. He plunked down a few coins as a different barkeep placed his drink before him. He knew that in all likelihood, the whiskey was nothing but moonshine, produced by the still in the cave outside of town near Hog Creek. He didn't taste it, only held it as he surveyed the room.

"Looking for a friend?" The girl who spoke at his elbow might have been young. It was hard to tell beneath the layers of makeup distorting her features. Her oily blond hair had been recently curled with a heated iron in lieu of washing, and her full figure was amply displayed by the plunging neckline of the dress she wore. Studying her, Stark had a sudden mental image of Prudence's warm loveliness. The tawdry cheapness of the girl beside him was abruptly repellant.

"Could be," he forced himself to answer her meaningless question. "Is that what you are? My friend?"

"Honey," she said in a husky voice, "I can be anything you want me to be." She moved closer to him. "What's your pleasure?"

Stark looked down into her painted face. "Just some talk for now. Maybe something else later."

"Well, all right. But not too much later, okay?" She raised her voice to the barkeep. "Jake, this man wants to buy me a drink. Don't you, honey?"

"Sure." Stark paid full price for what he was certain

was watered-down whiskey or plain tea. "I'm looking for a pal of mine," he told her as she took a miniscule sip of the pale liquid.

"Call me Janey," she said. "What's your pal's name?"

"Wills Bannister. I heard tell he was up in these parts. Old fella. Sound familiar?"

Her brow furrowed as she thought. "There used to be an old guy who hung around some. His name was Wills, or leastways something like that. He always had a story. To hear him tell it, he'd done everything from fighting Indians to hunting for lost treasure. He was a character, all right." She cocked her head up at Stark. "That sound like your pal?"

Stark's pulse quickened, but he forced himself to grin easily. "Sure does. He still around?"

Her dirty blond curls bounced as she shook her head. "Naw, I ain't seen him in a while." She frowned. "It's funny, but I don't know what happened to him. Seems like he was hanging around with some city dude, the last I saw him."

"City dude?" Stark prompted.

"Yeah," she said thoughtfully. "Young guy, kind of nice, but he got nervous in a saloon." Preoccupied with thought, some of the worldly cynicism fell away, revealing traces of a youthful prettiness that might still lurk beneath her painted exterior. "He'd come in and drag the old guy out when he got drunk."

"You know what happened to them? Where they went?"

Another shake of her head. "Naw, but that ain't unusual. Men come and go around here, ya know."

Slowly Stark became aware of movement near him, the shifting of bodies. Janey stiffened, and he found himself confronting a group of five men who had entered the saloon and loosely encircled him.

Three men dominated the group. To Stark's left was the yellow-haired fighter he'd seen brutalizing the cowhand in the ring as he rode in. The giant had donned a shirt and was apparently unarmed, but the savagery he had displayed in the fight still lurked in his wild eyes.

The man to Stark's right was of medium height and thin to the point of gauntness. His face was a collection of flat planes and harsh angles, pierced by eyes as cold and empty as the fighter's were wild. He wore a tailored suit, complete with vest and string tie. But everything about him—his stance, the placement of his hands, his coat neatly cut away so as not to impede his draw— seemed focused around the black revolver riding his hip in a nondescript leather holster. His thin lips lifted in a mirthless smile as his lifeless eyes met Stark's.

These two flanked the third man—tall, handsome, with a firm mouth below a patrician nose. He was so obviously the dominant personality among the group that the first two, formidable as they were, seemed inconsequential. His powerful body was clad in a stylish suit and whipcord trousers. A pearl-handled revolver was holstered at his side.

The remaining members of the quintet were nondescript hardcases—dangerous in their own right, but insignificant when compared to the others. The five stood in a loose semicircle, no one of them blocking another, so that Stark was effectively hemmed against the bar.

"Hello, Peacemaker," the leader said jovially, smiling to display even white teeth. "I've been hoping we'd meet, but the pleasure is more mine than yours, I'd wager. I'm Douglas Brockton."

It was obvious to Stark that they had been waiting for him. The barkeep who had first taken his order had apparently had a description of him and had gone to notify Brockton of his presence. It spoke disconcertingly of Brockton's power and influence in the town. Likely, every bartender in every establishment had been warned to be on the lookout for him.

Janey had shrunk back away from the group. A woman in her profession learned fast to read danger signs of tension between men, and she plainly read them now. From the look on her face, Stark was certain she hadn't been a part of the setup. With one last frightened glance at Stark, she slipped through the line of men and was gone, leaving him alone to face Brockton and his gang.

"I heard you looked like a shyster lawyer." Stark made the words an insult. "I guess that was right."

Brockton chuckled in apparent amusement. "That's because I spent a year in law school before I realized it was more lucrative to engage in dealings outside the law than to practice within it."

"Yes, you've done well for yourself," Stark said dryly. "Scrounging in this hellhole looking for your next deal."

The smile abruptly disappeared from the handsome face, as if it had been struck from a statue by a single blow of the chisel.

"I live well here, Stark," he said coldly, and then appeared to overcome his brief surge of anger. "But I suppose the delightful Miss Walker has painted an unflattering picture of me. She never did seem to warm to my attention. Where is she, by the way?"

"I sent her back to Guthrie after your thugs attacked us on the trail. By now she's there and under the protection of Evett Nix and his men."

"I strongly doubt that," Brockton said easily. "Instead I rather think she's hiding somewhere nearby in the company of your lovely wife. They shouldn't be that hard to find once we begin an earnest search." He paused theatrically, as if in a courtroom addressing a jury. "Of course, it occurs to me that I may not need her at all now that I have you."

"You don't have me yet," Stark said flatly.

Brockton chuckled once more. "Again I must disagree. Not only do I have you, but I'm certain you know the whereabouts of the item I'm seeking. Surely we can come to some sort of agreement."

"I doubt it."

"We'll see." Brockton seemed intent on continuing his farce of the polite gentleman entertaining a guest. "But first let me introduce you to my associates." He gestured grandly to the gaunt gunman. "Let me present Milo Hawk. Mr. Hawk has earned a certain reputation in these parts, not unjustified, I might add."

Closer scrutiny confirmed Stark's initial evaluation. Here was a professional, a true shootist, far removed from the gunslicks Brockton had sent up against him thus far. Hawk was a man to watch and to never underestimate.

"I've been wanting to meet you for a long time, Peacemaker." The gunman spoke in a deceptively mild tone. "Some who've seen us both in action think you can beat me to the draw. How about it, Stark? You think you can take me?"

The lines and angles of Hawk's face rearranged themselves in a hunter's grin. A cold fire had come to life deep down in his eyes. Stark didn't respond. He had the sudden feeling that anything he did, any move he made, might trigger this possessed man to go for his weapon. And, indeed, Hawk's hand had lifted to hover threateningly above the cutaway portion of his coat.

"And of course my other associate," said Brockton, sliding smoothly into the emotionally charged gap in the conversation. He indicated the prizefighter. "This is Spike Fennard. Spike has also earned himself quite a reputation. He has yet to be beaten in a bare knuckles contest. He likes to take on all-comers. I've seen him dispose of five men, one right after the other, and barely break a sweat."

Hawk had relaxed slightly, so Stark turned his attention to Fennard. Seen this close, the big man's blunt features bore the telltale marks of his profession. The broad nose had been broken more than once, the heavy brow was scarred, and age was showing in the lines around his eyes. An experienced bare knuckles fighter, just past his prime, Stark gauged him. But still very dangerous with his fists.

Douglas Brockton ran a hard crew.

Brockton hadn't bothered to introduce the other two men, but they didn't appear slighted by the fact. Their eyes, watchful and observant, remained on Stark. Whatever their failings as fighting men, when coupled with the likes of Brockton, Hawk, and Fennard, they completed a set of odds Stark knew he couldn't hope to oppose in an open gunfight. But would he have any other choice?

Brockton seemed to have followed Stark's mental process, for with a smug smile he proceeded to lay out another option. "I believe you and I need to talk, Peacemaker. But first I think there are certain, shall we say, preliminary negotiations which need to take place in order to firmly establish my bargaining position. In this case, I'm delegating these preliminary negotiations to my subordinate, Mr. Fennard."

A fight, Stark realized. Brockton intended to pit him against his pet brawler as the opening stages of whatever softening up process he had planned. But even if he won, Stark thought, there would be nothing for him save further brutality and mistreatment.

He glanced briefly over his shoulder. The burly barkeep who had betrayed him had reappeared. The man stood well back holding a sawed-off Greener shotgun leveled at Stark's back. Clearly he stood no chance if it came to gunplay.

Again Brockton might have read his thoughts. "I really think our entire relationship is on my terms."

Spike Fennard's eyes were alight with unnerving wildness. He grinned and began to unbutton his shirt. Stark noticed that the other patrons of the saloon had moved well away from the little drama that was unfolding. He glimpsed the anguished face of Janey, the bar girl, but there were no other signs of sympathy or support. Rather, the faces of most present showed only anticipation of a free show. He could expect no help from any quarter.

"Your gun, Stark," Brockton requested with exaggerated courtesy. "It really wouldn't be fair to leave you armed."

Stark had no choice but to go along with this and hope that during the fight he might get a chance to turn the tables. Reluctantly he unstrapped the holster and laid it on the bar behind him, where it was appropriated by the bartender.

Preparations were quickly made, leaving a large, cleared area with Stark and Fennard in the center of it. The fighter, stripped to the waist, stood leaning slightly forward, fists raised, like a savage dog restrained by a leash.

"I rather think we can dispense with the formalities, such as rounds," Brockton said from the sidelines. The leash had been loosed. Fennard came in hard.

Stark managed to get his guard up, but it did little good. Fennard's punishing left came straight through like a thunderbolt, snapping Stark's head around, setting off bells in his ears as if a gun had been fired too close. A hooking right followed fast, this time bouncing off his raised forearm, but still serving to drive him back. Again the left, which he managed to sidestep, leaving him open to the right coming in high overhand to rattle his teeth and set sparks dancing before his eyes.

Dimly, Stark realized this fight was already almost over if he didn't come up with a defensive strategy fast. His back came up hard against the bar, and he used it to brace himself and drive his fist straight out from his shoulder. He had the satisfaction of feeling it land solidly, of seeing it redden the skin of Fennard's cheek. But the big man only grinned as he pressed inexorably forward. Both fists hooked into Stark's midsection, hammering Stark's spine bruisingly back against the bar. Stark couldn't help dropping his arms reflexively, allowing Fennard's right to connect with his ear, spinning him along the bar clear of the bigger man's reach.

Face on fire, gut throbbing, legs threatening to collapse, Stark moved out into the open. He couldn't stand up to this man for long. But watching Fennard's confident pose, his posturing for the crowd, he thought he detected the glimmer of a chance.

Fennard was putting on an exhibition. He was used to taking on cowboys who fought barehanded mostly for fun, allowing Fennard to show off his skills to an admiring crowd. He wasn't used to fighting a skilled opponent whose sole goal was survival.

"Come on," Stark husked. "You haven't won yet."

Fennard's grin turned into a snarl. He put up his fists and danced in, light on his feet for all his bulk. Stark lifted his own hands, and as Fennard measured him, he lifted one foot and smashed the heel of his boot into the fighter's kneecap.

Pain and shock flared across the giant's face. His leg buckled slightly, and Stark hit him with a straight right that drove him staggering back. He caught his balance and the wildness in his eyes was replaced by blind fury. With a bellow of rage, he rushed, head down, like a bull.

But the injured leg betrayed him, and his charge became a stumbling lurch that Stark had no trouble pivoting away from. He put the pivot behind a blow, and his right hand came all the way around to drive his fist under Fennard's ear as the big man went by. Fennard's forward motion was converted into a shambling sidewise stagger.

Stark gave him no chance to recover. He hooked both hands to Fennard's skull, snapping his head first one way then the other, and drove a right directly between the addled eyes. Fennard might have fallen, but Stark, remembering the hapless cowpoke in the ring, ripped a left uppercut into his midriff that doubled him forward into a right uppercut that rocked his head back.

Stark stepped aside to let him fall. Fennard's face met the floor and he lay motionless. Stark's own legs were weak. The intense effort of the fight had drained him. Still he tried to turn as he heard the fast movement of feet behind him. But he was too slow. He felt the barrel of the gun crash down across the back of his neck with an agonizing jolt.

He didn't go completely out, but he was helpless as they manhandled him to his knees and bound his hands tightly behind him. He had a last glimpse of Janey's tearful face as he was hauled roughly to his feet.

The two nameless hardcases, with Milo Hawk in watchful attendance, escorted him down a hallway and shoved him into a small room with a single hard bunk. He recognized it as one of the cribs provided by the saloon for drunk patrons to sleep it off in relative safety. As a prison, he thought numbly, it served well.

Hawk stood over him where he had been shoved onto the bunk. "That was pretty good, Stark," the gunman admitted. "Fennard's been needing that done to him for a long time. And it let me see how good you are with your hands. You're fast, Stark, but I think I'm faster when it comes to a gun."

"There's a lot of men pushing up daisies who thought just like you do," Stark said with as much firmness as he could muster.

The man's only answer was a sneer.

"Milo, make sure we have a guard on this room. I don't want him getting loose." The voice belonged to Brockton who had appeared in the doorway. Hawk edged out of the room, leaving the two of them alone. "I have to say I'm impressed, Stark. But if you hadn't used your boot I don't think you could've taken him."

Stark shifted about until he could sit up on the bunk. The ropes binding his wrists behind him seemed secure. "I don't either," Stark admitted.

The man gave his amiable chuckle, then abruptly turned menacing. "Next time you won't have your hands free. And Spike won't be any too gentle after the way you beat him in front of his admiring fans."

"I imagine not."

"Actually, you could make it a lot easier on yourself by telling me now where the map is."

"Not to mention making it a lot easier on you. I don't think so, Brockton."

Brockton sighed expressively. "You're making a

mistake. You made one riding in here like you did. You're making another by not cooperating. I'll give you a while to think it over. And keep in mind, if Spike can't beat it out of you, I have an Apache brave who can do things to a human body with a knife that you wouldn't believe. Even Hawk doesn't care to watch him work."

When Stark didn't respond, Brockton did a slow circuit of the small room, an intense expression on his face. The man *was* a frustrated lawyer, Stark thought. He likely pictured himself with a skeptical client preparing to give astute legal advice. Stark could guess what was coming next.

"Actually," Brockton began, "I'm sorry that we have to be at odds like this. Two intelligent men like us—both professionals in our own way—should be able to reach some kind of mutually acceptable agreement." He paused as if to let his words sink in. "In fact, I believe something in the way of a partnership might be in order if we could come to terms."

Stark decided to ask. "What kind of terms?"

Immediate satisfaction flashed onto Brockton's face. "I think a partnership demands a gesture of good faith from both partners. In this case, your gesture would be turning the map over to me."

"And your gesture?"

Brockton was sure of himself now. "Why, you could accompany us to the mountains and share in the treasure." His face was alive with passion. "Think of it, Stark! All that gold just waiting to be taken. It must be worth over a million dollars by now. We could pay off the hired help like Hawk and split it. What would you do with that much gold, Peacemaker?"

Stark started to tell him to forget the offer, but resisted the impulse. There was no point in hurrying whatever unpleasantries Brockton might have in store for him.

Brockton seemed willing to let it ride also. The avarice in his eyes was replaced by practicality. "I'll leave you to think it over. But don't try my patience. I won't wait forever."

Stark heard the click of a bolt as the door closed behind his captor. He shifted again on the bunk and stared at his prison. He remembered his earlier defiant words to Brockton. They were no longer true. Brockton did, indeed, have him now.

Chapter Six

Where was Jim? What had happened to him? The questions echoed endlessly in Prudence's mind.

For what seemed the hundredth time she rose from her bedroll where she had been restlessly dozing and prowled the tiny smokeless camp Jim had made for them. He had told her he planned on returning before dark and now it was not too far from dawn.

Her eyes had long since grown accustomed to the darkness and her nerves had stopped jumping at every sound from the black wall of surrounding woods. But images persisted in forming in her mind, images which refused to let her rest. The decision to go into town after him had been a subtle one, settling into her mind before she was even quite aware that it had become a firm commitment. But now that the decision had been made, she wasted no more time.

She roused Sarah and told her of her intentions. In the lessening gloom, the girl's fear and confusion was obvious. But like Prudence, she too seemed to accept that something had gone dreadfully wrong for Stark and it was up to them to right it.

They caught their horses and saddled them. Then together they repacked their bedrolls and the few other items they'd used and moved the heavy packs into the trees at the edge of the clearing, close to where the packhorse was grazing. Everything now was ready to be quickly loaded when they returned with Stark.

If they returned, Prudence amended ruefully.

Resolutely she checked her revolver and rifle, and watched as Sarah nervously did the same. Then they rode out. It took several minutes of negotiating between tree trunks and ducking shadowy branches in the dark before they emerged from the wooded draw which concealed the camp. The grassland stretched before them in eerie shades of black and gray.

Possessed by the sense of urgency, Prudence put her mare into a gallop and set a brisk pace for town. The glow of lights guided her as they drew near. She reined up in sight of the ramshackle collection of shanties on the outskirts of town that housed the town's permanent inhabitants.

Sarah's eyes immediately settled on a sagging shack set slightly apart from the others. The sloping roof had collapsed on one corner, and the sagging door, held on by only one hinge, bore a relatively fresh coat of whitewash.

There was excitement in her hushed whisper. "From the description in Timothy's letter, that has to be the cabin where the map is hidden. He specifically mentioned the door."

Prudence had thus far been operating without a plan, but with this revelation a course of action came to mind. She made a hurried decision. "I think we should split up. If I do manage to locate Jim, we'll have to make a hurried escape from town. There won't be time to go after the map then. Why don't you retrieve it, then wait for us here on this rise."

"But you might need me to help rescue Mr. Stark," the girl protested.

"That's true in one sense," Prudence agreed. "But we must keep the overall goal of the mission in mind. Without that map, we're defeated before we even start. Brockton will eventually start dismantling the town building by building and come up with the map on his own. We can't let him find it . . . and we can't risk him getting hold of you either. This way we stand a chance of retrieving the map and keeping you out of his hands as well."

Sarah seemed ready to protest, then thought better of it. She nodded mutely. "Please be careful," she pleaded.

"You too." For the first time the hopelessness of the situation settled fully upon Prudence. If she failed in her rescue of Jim, the girl was doomed. She thought of instructing Sarah to head for Liberal, Kansas if they weren't back by a certain time. But in the end she decided it would be a waste of breath and time.

A failed rescue would alert Brockton and loose a man-hunt for Sarah that would net the girl within hours if not minutes. There was only one solution. She couldn't fail.

She wouldn't fail, she vowed, urging her mare forward.

There was no sign of life as Sarah eased her horse in among the outermost structures. Timothy's sketchy description in his letters did little to prepare her for the rotting crumbling reality through which she rode. The stench of garbage and waste assailed her nostrils.

A light gust of wind banged a shutter on a deserted hut as she passed, setting her heart to pounding. Her horse shied away from a dark shape on the ground, and she realized that the motionless form was human. Alive or dead, she couldn't tell. She guided the animal around it without stopping to ascertain.

She halted her horse in the shadows of the sagging shack she had chosen as her target and listened intently. From the main part of town came a faint drunken yell and several gunshots. In reflex her hand tightened convulsively on the reins. There was no nearby alarm, and she relaxed slightly. Apparently such outbreaks were so commonplace here they caused no reaction.

It took a distinct physical effort for her to dismount, and once on foot she was reluctant to leave her horse and the scant measure of security the animal provided.

She drew her revolver as she started forward. The shack was supposed to be deserted, but some time had passed since Timothy had written his letter.

The door sagged open on its single hinge. Peering inside, she could make out a jumble of unidentifiable shapes. Cautiously, she entered. Once safely inside, she holstered her revolver long enough to light a candle she had brought for the purpose. Her hands were shaking so badly it seemed to take an eternity to accomplish the task.

The flickering flame revealed shabby furniture in various stages of disrepair. A massive wooden wardrobe stood against one wall, the only piece in the one-room cabin that was anything other than junk.

She threaded her way among the debris to the far corner of the room near the wardrobe. Setting the candle down carefully, she knelt beside it. Her probing fingers quickly found the loose floorboard, and she lifted it easily. Her breath was coming rapidly as she reached into the dark void, all fear of rats and other vermin displaced by her need to secure her prize.

She drew out an oilskin packet and gripped it tightly in both hands, resisting the urge to hug it to herself in the thrill of the moment.

"What'd ya find, little lady?" The rough, masculine voice from the doorway jolted her.

She whirled about as she came to her feet. The candle's uncertain light revealed a large man filling the entrance. Flickering shadows darted across the sagging features, split by a gaping toothless mouth.

Sarah caught her breath, feeling as if a vise was constricting her chest. She could only stare helplessly as the huge man stepped into the shack. Even from a distance, his foul odor assaulted her senses.

"Durned if Mr. Brockton wasn't right," the hoarse voice continued. "He said with that highpowered gunslick locked up it might pay to watch ol' Bannister's shack. And sure enough, here you come, traipsing right along into the trap. Ain't that something?" He grinned horribly, the gleam of saliva drooling down his fleshy chin.

"I'll bet you for sure found whatever it was Mr. Brockton's been looking for, right?" His chuckle was a liquid rasp. "Mr. Brockton'll be real happy when I bring it to him. But first, I think you and me oughta have a little celebration." He took a shambling step forward.

The threatening movement galvanized her to action. She fumbled for the revolver with her right hand. As a draw, it left a lot to be desired, but she got the weapon free and had the satisfaction of seeing her would-be suitor flinch back in sudden fear. Instinctively her finger tightened on the trigger and the sharp crack of the gun seemed to split her ears.

The drunken rowdy let out a howl and scrambled for the door. She fired again, barely realizing what she was doing. Then the burly man was out the door and lost in the darkness, and she was left trembling in shock and horror.

"Ya missed me, little lady," came the ghastly voice. "Scared me a mite, though. I'll have to make ya pay for that."

Sarah bit back the scream that rose in her throat. It would do no good to scream. Frantically she looked about for another exit, but there was no way out except the door she'd entered.

"Ya ready for me, little lady? I'm coming back in."

Abruptly the door slammed back against the wall. Sarah's finger jerked the trigger, kept jerking it, the shots rolling one after another in the small confines of the shack.

With an effort she managed to control her fear, realizing he'd slammed the sagging door from outside, tricking her into wasting ammunition. The thought of being outwitted by the monstrous oaf sparked anger within her.

"That was six, little lady. You're all outta bullets now. Time for you and me to have some fun!"

Sarah's darting eyes settled on the wardrobe. There was just room between it and the wall for her to slide behind it. After a moment she heard the sound of his shambling footsteps and panting breath.

"Where'd ya go, little lady?" His voice sounded horribly near. "You may as well come on out and give me what I want." The sounds of his approach were unmistakable.

Sarah took a deep breath, and now that the moment was upon her stepped out from behind the wardrobe and quite coolly shot him in the chest with the final bullet in her seven-shot revolver.

He staggered at the impact and shock registered on his brutish features. As his knees buckled, she slipped past him and darted from the shack, not looking behind her as she went. She scrambled aboard her horse, at any moment expecting to feel his groping hand on her ankle. But he didn't appear, so her single shot, whether or not fatal, must have been incapacitating.

Trembling, she forced her thoughts away from the fact that she might have killed a man. She had no choice. She shuddered again at the fate she had narrowly escaped. She had acted in self-defense.

She had acted . . .

Somewhere in the back of her mind, Prudence's words echoed joltingly. She had had the courage to act when the situation warranted it . . . even despite her fear.

Prudence. She hoped by now the woman had located her beloved Jim. The drunken oaf had all but said Stark was being held captive by Brockton somewhere in this hellhole of a town. Oh, well, if anyone could succeed in such a mission, it was Prudence Stark.

Sarah quickly voiced a silent prayer for her new friends and protectors. She knew all too well she stood little chance of survival without them. But her concern went well beyond selfishness. She had come to care deeply about the Starks during their short association.

Again she fought down the fear and mustered her courage. Instead of putting her horse into a dead run out of town as she so longed to do, she kept to the backs of buildings and headed out toward the spot where she was to rendezvous with the pair. They would be there shortly. She just knew they would.

Prudence froze as she heard the gunshots coming from the direction of the cabin where Sarah was searching for the map. If they concerned Sarah, she could only hope the girl was able to escape the danger on her own. She forced her attention back to her own mission. She had to concentrate or all was lost. Time to mount a rescue of Sarah later, if one proved necessary, when Jim was again at her side.

The sky was definitely growing lighter and with the coming of dawn her chances of being detected greatly increased. She thought achingly of Stark, wishing desperately for his presence, his easy competence in situations such as this. *Please, Lord*, she prayed, barely realizing she was doing so. *Please let me find him.*

She urged her mare across a side street and into yet another narrow filthy alley that continued to parallel the main street. The building she was passing, apparently a saloon from the odors of liquor emanating from it, had a makeshift corral built behind it. Probably, she guessed, it was for the convenience of regular patrons who wouldn't want to leave their animals tied out front for extended periods.

A flicker of movement inside the corral caught her eye. For a moment she thought the predawn light was playing tricks on her vision. Then the big sorrel stallion, as if scenting her presence, gave a low whinny and broke free from the rest of the stock to trot eagerly to the fence.

"Red!" she exclaimed in delight. She dismounted and gave the stallion a rewarding pat on the neck for alerting her.

The horse was still saddled and bridled, she saw. Whoever had turned him in with the other horses had likely done so to appropriate the animal rather than out of any sense of kindness.

"I'll find him, fella," she whispered and turned to look at the building.

Her initial elation faded at the prospect of entering the place. But she'd come this far and couldn't give up now. She tied her mare to the corral, then crossed the alley to the back door. It was unlocked and opened into a deserted storage area.

She drew her revolver and tiptoed across the room to emerge in a dim corridor. She could see the shadowy outline of stairs at the end. Upstairs would be where the prostitutes plied their trade. Surely if Jim was imprisoned here, it wouldn't be up there.

She froze as the sound of footsteps sounded on the stairs. For an instant she stood paralyzed, undecided whether to run or duck back into the storage area. The next moment she found herself facing a young blond woman on the stairs.

"Who are you?" the blond gasped as her startled gaze took in Prudence and the drawn revolver.

The woman was pretty, her face scrubbed clean of makeup. She wore a tattered red robe, which she held closed at the neckline. Prudence watched as fright faded to understanding.

The blond descended another step, staring hard at her. "You're with him, aren't you?"

Prudence finally found her voice. "What do you mean?" she demanded. "Who do you think I am?"

The blond came the rest of the way down the staircase. "You're riding with that man Mr. Brockton's men roughed up."

"James Stark?"

The blond nodded. "Yeah. They called him something else too . . ."

"The Peacemaker," Prudence guessed, and the girl's nod confirmed it. "Where is he?" She fought the urge to grab the girl and shake her into cooperation.

"Down there." She pointed past Prudence's shoulder. "They got him locked up."

"Is he all right? Did they hurt him?"

"They worked him over some. But first he beat the devil out of Spike Fennard, a professional fighter Mr. Brockton sicced on him." Her eyes lit with a muted pleasure. "My name's Janey. I was just going to check on Mr. Stark. He's different from the other men around here."

"Yes, he is," Prudence agreed with a note of pride. "Will you help me get him out?"

Janey clearly wavered, her face contorted by an expression of near physical pain. Then she nodded. "Yes. But we need to hurry. Come on." She caught Prudence's hand in a grip so tight it hurt and pulled her down the hall.

Then they heard the unmistakable sound of footsteps and voices approaching from around the corner.

"It's Mr. Brockton!" Janey gasped, her expression one of white-faced terror. Still gripping Prudence's hand, she hauled her across the hallway and through another door, easing it shut to a crack. In the darkness, the room smelled of dust and stale provisions—possibly a storage room.

They huddled together, and Prudence realized Janey was shaking. She wondered numbly what experiences the girl had undergone with Brockton to instill such fear.

"I've got some business upstairs, then I'm going to get a few hours sleep," Brockton was telling his companion as they came around the corner. "After that, I'll talk to Stark again. If he doesn't cooperate, you and the boys can have another go at him."

Through the cracked door, Prudence glimpsed a handsome man accompanied by a blond giant who appeared to be limping.

"I don't need nobody's help!" the big man protested angrily.

"Just remember yesterday," Brockton retorted sharply. "Look at you. You're all but crippled now."

His companion's surly response was lost as they ascended the stairs. After a moment Janey opened the door and hurriedly led Prudence back to the corner to peer down the intersecting hallway.

"There's a guard outside his door," Janey hissed in frustration. She grew thoughtful, then proposed, "I'll lead the guard away. Then you can get in there and get Mr. Stark out."

"But what about you?" Prudence felt compelled to ask. "Will you be all right?"

Janey nodded. "Yeah, the other girls will cover for me. And if the guard says anything, it'll be his neck too! Now give me five minutes."

It actually didn't take more than three, Prudence guessed, although the time seemed an eternity to her. She heard Janey's voice, and deeper tones as the man answered. Whatever proposal Janey made to him must have been quickly accepted. She heard their footsteps recede, and when she risked a look down the hallway they had disappeared.

She rushed to the locked door and slipped the bolt. When she peered inside, her gaze fell on an empty bunk. At the same instant, the door was jerked open and a partially-pulled blow glanced off her shoulder. From behind the door where he waited to ambush who-ever entered the room, James Stark stared at her in bewilderment.

"Jim!" she gasped. "You're okay. Thank God!" She flew into his arms, forgetting the danger and the per-ilous situation.

He held her to him for an instant then thrust her urgently away. "What are you doing here?"

She saw his face bore the unmistakable scars of a

beating, and his wrists were horribly scraped from escaping his bonds. She stretched up and tenderly kissed one of the bruises. "I came to find you. I knew something was wrong."

He didn't waste time with any more questions. He appropriated her revolver and slipped out into the hallway. Then with a growl of disbelief, he handed the gun back to her and snatched his own holster from where it had been hung on a peg outside his cell as though it was a trophy.

Prudence felt a sense of relief in yielding to his control as he strapped the Colt Peacemaker in place. "The horses are out back," she told him. "Someone had turned Red into the corral behind this dreadful place."

He nodded. "All right. Let's go." He drew his gun and led the way swiftly down the hall.

Prudence thought briefly of Janey, but there was no way to take the girl with them, should she even be willing to go.

As they turned the corner, Stark drew up sharply.

"What the devil?" came the startled voice of Douglas Brockton. From the bottom of the stairs, Brockton went fast for his gun.

Stark's arm snapped out so quickly Prudence couldn't see the movement, and the revolver cracked in his fist. Brockton cried out in pain and grabbed his shoulder as he fell back against the stairs.

Stark rushed across the empty storeroom and out the back door, his grip on Prudence's wrist pulling her along in his wake. Behind them they heard Brockton's outraged bellow for help as they burst outside. Stark was at the corral gate and through it by the time Prudence mounted her mare.

He swung aboard Red and pulled his repeating shotgun from its sheath. One-handed, he flipped it in the air to work the lever, and it spat flame at the first startled face to appear in the doorway. He urged Red through the gate on the heels of a half dozen other frantic animals he drove before him.

Then they were racing down the alley in the midst of the other horses. In a matter of moments, they pounded past the outskirts of town, leaving the last of the freed horses behind them.

"Sarah should be waiting for us just ahead on that rise," Prudence shouted above the drumming of hoofbeats.

As if on cue, the girl appeared out of a meager fringe of trees and swung in beside them as they raced on across the grassland beneath the lightening sky.

"I got the map!" Sarah informed them triumphantly.

Stark grinned first at the girl then at Prudence and let out a whoop of joy that brought an exultant smile to Prudence's face in response.

Maybe the aura of doom that had cloaked this mission from the beginning had finally been dispelled, she thought with a surge of gratitude for answered prayer.

Chapter Seven

"We can stop to rest the horses a few minutes, but no longer," Stark told the women.

He didn't like the idea, but knew it was a necessity. Sarah's horse and the packhorse were clearly wearing down. Even Red and Prudence's mare were beginning to show the strain of the punishing pace Stark had set throughout the morning. They had ridden hard and fast after leaving White City, pausing only minutes at the campsite to pick up the packhorse and their supplies.

They dismounted in the shelter of a band of woods flanking a narrow creek. There had been no sign of pursuit, but Stark didn't want to relax his caution. He'd gained a grudging respect for the relentless cunning of the man who opposed them.

"Never mind the horses," Sarah said with feeling. "*I* need the rest." She knelt beside the stream and cupped both hands to drink.

Stark himself was feeling the effects of his ordeal. They had managed in snatches during their hectic ride to exchange stories. He now felt a healthy gratitude for the women's courage in riding into White City to retrieve the map and rescue him. Even after he'd gotten his hands free, he knew his escape was anything but certain.

Prudence dropped her mare's reins, and the horse waded out ankle deep into the stream to drink. She then came to slip into the protective circle of Stark's arm as he allowed Red to do the same. She looked up searchingly into his eyes. "Are you okay?"

He nodded. "I'm getting there." He pulled her close and pressed his lips to her forehead, causing Sarah to look away in embarrassment. He took the opportunity to bring the girl into the conversation. "Sarah, I found out that apparently Timothy and Bannister did manage to slip out without Brockton knowing."

The girl's face brightened. "Really?"

"Yep. I talked to someone who said the two of them were there, then all of a sudden they were gone. And this person would've known if Brockton had had anything to do with their disappearance."

Prudence glanced up sharply. "You mean Janey?" At his nod, she continued. "She helped by distracting your guard so I could get you out. We owe her a lot."

He nodded again. "After this is over, we'll find some way to pay her back . . . help her get out of there. And a place to start helping her is by defeating Brockton. He's got that whole town and everyone in it under his thumb. You ladies ready to move out?"

He saw renewed conviction settle on their faces as they mounted their horses. It was best to be on their way. He wasn't certain how badly he'd wounded Brockton, but he knew the man wouldn't give up the chase once he was back on his feet. He wanted to establish as big a lead as possible as they headed southeast toward the Wichita Mountains and the mystery they held.

They pushed on relentlessly for three days, their short nights spent in exhausted slumber. But late on the fourth day he called an early halt in a gentle draw beneath a large solitary tree.

"I think it's time we took a good look at this mysterious map," he told the women.

Excitement danced in Sarah's eyes. Their earlier examinations of her find had been, of necessity, cursory. After the horses were cared for, she hurriedly withdrew the oilskin packet from her saddlebag and spread the contents out before them.

"I recognize this as the original map Timothy discovered," she told them as she unrolled the small tapestry. "He must've made a copy of it for himself."

"Maybe he wasn't sure he and Bannister could get away from Brockton and they didn't want to risk losing the original," Prudence proposed.

Stark nodded. It was irrelevant why Timothy had chosen to leave the map. He was just glad they had it. At this point, they needed every break they could get. Stark knew the tale of the mysterious Mexican who wore the silk map around his waist beneath his clothes, and this aged cloth certainly fit the description.

Recalling Sarah's story of how Timothy Rankin had found it among the possessions of an elderly deceased Mexican, he wondered if that man had indeed been the one who had roamed the territory in a fruitless quest for the cave with its enigmatic iron door.

The map was some five feet by two feet with ragged edges. The material was worn thin along the creases where it had long been folded. A maze of lines and curves had been drawn to depict some portion of the Wichita Mountains, with a picture of what was meant to be an iron door marking one point of a canyon.

Along the tapestry's ragged edges were sketches of

various sites, apparently corresponding to numbered points on the map. The artwork, while simple, conveyed scenes with startling clarity despite the faded colors.

"This looks like three hills close to where you enter the mountains," Sarah said eagerly, jabbing an emphatic finger at the first drawing. And what's this?" she indicated the next one.

Prudence studied the scene. "It looks like a tree with a spike of some sort driven in it. Maybe at the mouth of a canyon."

"Yes!" Sarah cried in excitement. "And the other drawings are just as easy to decipher. I know we can follow them to the cave!"

Stark didn't share her optimism. "Remember, according to the tale, the original owner of this map spent years trying to locate the treasure. Even with it in hand he couldn't do so."

"But the other expedition found it!" Sarah insisted. "Wills Bannister said so. And they were using a copy of this map."

"I suppose you expect Timothy to be there at the iron door waiting for us?" Stark asked in a mildly mocking tone.

Sarah's excitement died at his sobering question. "I don't know where Timothy is. But I do know he was trying to follow this map. Following it ourselves is our best chance of finding him."

Prudence frowned a reprimand, and Stark sighed. "Sorry." He rubbed his neck in frustration. His impatience with the girl's naivete was simply a lingering effect of the fight with Fennard, he told himself. "We just need to be careful," he finished lamely. "A lot of people have died looking for this gold."

And he had almost joined their number, he thought ruefully.

Prudence seemed ready to move the conversation back to the map. "Look," she said softly, pointing to the last image on the tapestry. "What do you suppose this means?"

It was a carefully drawn skull, and the dark eye sockets seemed to peer intently at Stark. "Some sort of warning, I expect," he ventured. "It's right next to a drawing of the iron door. Maybe it has to do with the Indians the Spaniards entombed with the gold."

On that somber note, Prudence dropped to her knees beside Sarah and began folding the map.

Sarah didn't object. It was as if she were relieved to put away the evil it portended—at least for the evening. She ran her hand caressingly over the fabric one last time before she rose. "I wonder where it came from. Who made it, I mean."

"Maybe it was made by one of the Spaniards who was on the original expedition that mined the gold." Stark realized that at some point he had come to unconsciously accept the reality of the lost cave . . . and the authenticity of the map. "It's conceivable that at least one of them stayed on this continent in hopes of returning to retrieve the gold. In that case, the map could have been passed down from father to son. The Mexican who owned it might well have been a descendant of that original conquistador."

Prudence looked up at Stark as if in agreement with him, then her eyes darted past him and widened in shock.

Stark spun around, the Colt Peacemaker clearing leather as he turned. He found himself confronting an ancient Indian brave standing a little above him on the lip of the draw. Stark realized he'd been absorbed in the map, but still it didn't seem possible that this elderly man could have approached to within ten feet without him being aware of it.

And the old Indian was apparently traveling this sea of grass *on foot*. There was no sign of a horse—only the solitary figure regarding them with shrewd black eyes from a parchment face.

Sarah was staring wide-eyed. "Who is he?"

Stark didn't answer, for he saw the Indian's attention was focused not on them but on the map Prudence was carefully folding. Slowly he holstered his gun. "You know this map, old one?"

After a long pause, the ancient nodded. "I know of it," he answered in a surprisingly deep voice.

The old man's long mane of hair was silver now, instead of its original black. A beaded headband encircled his forehead, and with something of a shock, Stark saw he was armed with the traditional weapons of his people. An unstrung bow was carried across his back, and a knife and a hand-fashioned axe were slung at his waist.

"You travel alone, Father." Stark made it a statement.

Again the nod. "I have been alone for many years now. It is better this way."

"You would share our food with us?" This time Stark made the invitation a question. "We would learn from your wisdom."

It was the right approach. The old warrior gave his nod and came stiffly down the slight slope to the camp. He sat in stoic silence as they set out provisions. He ate the bacon and biscuits with strong brown teeth and grunted his appreciation. The women followed Stark's lead and ate in silence out of respect for the old man's very presence, as dictated by his culture.

"You search for the gold," he said at last after drawing the back of one leathery hand across his mouth.

"We follow the map," Stark said carefully. "The young woman's betrothed disappeared looking for the gold. We seek to find him."

"You search for the gold," the Indian repeated, as if his statement had been confirmed.

"If the gold is there, we will perhaps find it," Stark conceded. "What do you know of the map? Does it truly show where the gold is hidden?"

"So they say." For the first time a dark emotion flared in the onyx eyes. "It is an evil thing," he said with abrupt vehemence. "It should be destroyed."

Dread raced up Stark's spine. "Who made this map, old one?"

"It is said that one of the Golden Ones did. I have never seen it before this day, but I know it is evil— tainted by the deaths of many who have gone before."

"Who are the Golden Ones?" Stark prodded gently.

The old man closed his eyes and bowed his head for a long moment. When at last he looked up, his eyes seemed to gaze beyond their little camp into the vast unfathomable distance. "Many years ago my people lived in those mountains. We had a good way of life until the strangers came. We called them the Golden Ones because they sought gold with their very souls . . . and because the sunlight made their armor shine like the gold they sought."

Watching him, listening to him, Stark had the sudden impression that he was hearing a tale recounted by one who had actually seen the things he described, had participated in the events he spoke of. But of course that was nonsense. The coming of the Spanish conquistadors to the territory had been well over a century before.

"The Golden Ones made slaves of my people and forced them to dig for the gold. Then they melted it into bars and stored it in a cave guarded by a massive door of iron. After many years, my people could stand no more. They turned on the Golden Ones and killed many of them until the rest fled our lands, leaving their gold behind them. But before they went they did two things. They slaughtered those of our people who had been forced to help them and locked their bodies up with the gold."

"And the other thing?" Stark asked.

"They left the spirits of those we killed to watch over the gold and prevent us from ever removing the bodies of our people from that cursed place. From that day, my people have stayed away from that part of the mountains, driven away by the spirits of the Golden Ones. And as of old, they have taken some of our people to serve them even to this day."

The dark eyes came back from wherever they had been and focused intently on Stark. "That is why I say the map you carry is evil. It shows you only the way to death by the spirits of the Golden Ones."

"Do you know anything of two men, one old, one young, who went into the mountains some moons ago to look for the gold?" Stark asked. "They carried a map like this."

"Many white men have gone into the mountains looking for the gold. Few have ever returned. As to what happened to those you seek, who can say? I have told you what I know."

Stark glanced at Sarah and saw the strange haunted look in her eyes. He knew the old brave's words had been difficult for her to hear. "You will stay with us tonight, Father?"

"No," the old man said flatly as he rose to his feet.

"But it is growing dark," he protested, rising himself. If convinced to stay, he knew the old man might well be led to reveal significant details about the mountains and the lost cave.

But the ancient brave was already striding away from

the camp. "The darkness and I are friends," he called in parting.

Prudence was suddenly on her feet beside Stark. She made a motion as if to add her objections to his, but then she seemed to think better of it. She let her hand fall back to her side.

Meanwhile, the old man disappeared into the dusk, and Stark felt a sudden need to replenish the fire. Night seemed to be falling with startling swiftness.

"What do you think he meant by the Golden Ones?" Sarah asked in a small voice.

Stark continued to stare toward the spot where the old man had vanished. "Indian legend," he said after a moment. "Probably fabricated to explain why his people shun the area."

"But if the Indians avoid the area around the cave, then who chased off Bannister's expedition?" Prudence asked with her often maddening lawyer's logic.

This time it seemed more maddening than usual. He remembered the eerie drawing of the skull on the map, the words of Ramirez back in Guthrie, the warning of the old brave . . .

"I don't know," he said honestly. "Maybe the spirits of the Golden Ones."

In that moment with the darkness fast gathering about them and the presence of the ancient Indian seeming to hover over them, Stark almost believed the statement himself.

Chapter Eight

The Wichita Mountains in the southwestern part of Oklahoma Territory were a maze of rugged wooded hills, blind canyons, and jagged weathered rock. Stark had seen the Rockies, and compared to that vast range the Wichitas were little more than foothills. But they possessed a unique brooding character all their own.

For centuries the hills had served as refuge for those hunted by others. Indian tribes, some vanished altogether now, had fled other stronger tribes and then lured their enemies into the rugged landscape to fall prey to ambush. Outlaws and desperados had set up enclaves there from which to sally forth and ravage and pillage the territory.

The desperation and violence of all those hunted men must have somehow permeated the very stones of these hills, Stark thought. How else could he explain the unnerving sense of wariness that rode him like a dark spirit as they penetrated the maze of draws and canyons? He remembered the words of the old Indian, and the sun beating down seemed a shade cooler to him.

"You've been here before, haven't you?" Sarah

asked as they halted to sip from their canteens in the shadow of a large rock.

"Yes, often," Stark acknowledged. "But nobody really knows all these hills. It's easy to get turned around and lose your way even if you're familiar with the area. That's why the cave has remained lost all these years. Those who see it are unable to find their way back after they leave."

As he spoke, he realized once more that he had accepted the reality of the cave and its contents.

"The three hills marked on the map could be anywhere in this mountain range," he went on. "But I think I know a good place to start looking."

The peak he sought was one of the highest in the range. He remembered it as a lookout site used by outlaws to spot pursuers, and by bounty hunters, such as himself, to look for traces of their quarry. Sarah remained silent as they rode, the lines of her jaw taut and hard. It was as if, upon having finally reached the mountains, she expected the cave to be there in front of them in plain sight. Irrational as it was, she obviously resented the fact that it wasn't.

He spotted the lookout point shortly. The circuitous route to the top necessitated leaving the packhorse tethered to graze at its base. On the way up, Stark pointed out a family of bighorn sheep bounding from crag to crag with casual grace on an opposite cliff face. From the summit of the peak, the mountainous terrain spread out before them in a jagged maze of earth tones and green.

Sarah caught her breath. "I had no idea it was like this. It's so jumbled, so desolate and lost . . ."

"Yeah," Prudence sighed. "It hasn't been that long since I was here, and even I didn't remember it being quite so wild."

Stark said nothing. He had long ago grown used to the wildness of these mountains. Still, seeing them again now after some years, he felt a quickening of his pulse, a heightening of his senses. Some ancient upheaval must have thrust these rough stony bulwarks up from the plains. And in the eons since that time, the weather and natural forces had combined to erode and work the pitiless stone into a natural labyrinth of canyons, cliffs, and caves.

With the binoculars he did a slow sweep, but saw no signs of human life. Sarah, without being prompted, had withdrawn the map from its packet and partially unfolded it on a rock. Stark and Prudence knelt beside her to study the first drawing on the map. Three mountains were clearly depicted. Two were of equal height. The one on the left was the tallest and green in color, evidently indicating a heavy growth of forest.

With his naked eye, Stark studied the surrounding terrain, aware that the women were doing the same.

"There!" Sarah cried suddenly and pointed.

For a moment Stark didn't see the mountains she'd indicated. Then his eyes fell on one peak clothed in evergreens, and the next instant he spotted the two smaller hills adjacent to it. He lifted the binoculars and studied the trio of hills. They were reversed from the drawing, as if the artist had been on the other side of the hills and a little south of their current position. But the resemblance was unmistakable.

"That's it," he confirmed. "Let's go."

Negotiating the rugged terrain to the approximate location of the sketch site took the rest of the afternoon. They camped that night in a rocky defile, and by the light of the fire they once again examined the map.

"Tomorrow we need to look for the tree with the spike driven in it," Sarah announced excitedly.

Prudence smiled over at the girl. "That's right. We're one step closer."

"We'll have to keep watch tonight," Stark told them. "I don't trust these hills." In truth, they had seen no signs of other humans throughout the long day—only the slither of reptiles, the scurrying of small mammals, the distant shape of a vulture soaring far ahead. But the feeling of wariness persisted in Stark. Indian folklore aside, these hills were undoubtedly still home to desperate lawless men who, given the opportunity, would kill them and take whatever they desired with callous ease.

And somewhere behind them a vengeful Douglas Brockton would by now be on the move.

But the night was uneventful, and the morning was spent in a fruitless frustrating search for a tree with a spike, presumably a mark left by the Spaniards to allow them to return at a later date.

"It's got to be here!" Sarah said impatiently from atop a tall boulder where she had scrambled to better survey the area.

"The map is over a century old," Prudence reminded her. "That's a long time for a tree or anything else to exist."

Sarah scowled darkly and didn't answer.

In the end it was Stark who discovered the ancient gnarled oak over the next rise. The tree had grown through the decades so that the metal head of the spike was now flush with the bark of the tree. He'd almost overlooked it, but the tree was located at the mouth of a narrow canyon exactly as the sketch depicted. He had examined it closely just for that reason.

The canyon snaked back ever deeper into the mountains. Rather than travel its sandy floor, Stark insisted they follow the rim. The narrow confines of the canyon were a perfect setup for an ambush site. Sarah obviously resented the delay, but didn't argue.

Late afternoon brought them to the lip of a hundred-foot drop from which they could see a mammoth black opening in the far wall of the canyon. If the map proved accurate, this cave was nowhere near the treasure cave, but Stark felt obliged to investigate further.

In the hours before dark they descended to the canyon floor and approached the cave mouth. Closer inspection revealed not so much a cave as a sheltered area beneath a massive rock overhang. Apparently it had been hollowed out by the rush of water down the canyon over the centuries.

They had left the horses on the canyon rim, but Stark had brought a lantern for just this purpose. With it lit, they ventured under the overhanging mass of stone into the darkness there. The recess was some fifty or sixty feet deep, and at the very back Stark had to duck as his Stetson brushed the stone roof.

The dancing lantern flame played over faded images of men with spears stalking great bison-like creatures across the stone wall. The drawings were not detailed, but they possessed a flowing symmetry that hinted at the reality behind them. In the uncertain light, the ancient hunters and their prey seemed actually to move across their stone landscape with mesmerizing beauty.

"The people of that old brave who came to our camp must have done these drawings," Sarah said in awe.

"Or their ancestors," Stark confirmed. "These are old. They were here long before the Spaniards ever came to these mountains looking for gold."

Prudence moved closer to Stark for a better look and her foot hit something buried in the sand. "What's this?"

Stark used his boot to brush aside the sand. The

lantern light revealed an ancient longsword, the blade broken near the point.

"It's Spanish!" Sarah exclaimed. "I've seen pictures in Timothy's books. This proves the Spaniards were here!" She knelt to feel around in the sand. Her scrabbling fingers uncovered another item, this one rounded. With some effort, she pulled a metal helmet from the sand. It was unmistakably the distinctive headgear of the conquistadors.

Bending, Stark picked up the sword. Like the helmet, it was old—not as old as the cave paintings, of course— but pitted and corroded by the passage of time. He hefted the weapon, the blade broken in some long forgotten fray. It would've been a formidable instrument of death in the hands of one trained to use it.

Briefly he considered taking it with him. But suddenly in his mind's eye he saw the image of the weapon's owner, crouched here studying the cave paintings in some long ago year. The idea died stillborn. Somehow these weapons belonged here in this place.

Sarah must have experienced something of the same sensation, for she abruptly placed the helmet back on the sandy floor. "I wonder how they got here?"

"We can only guess at that," Prudence said resignedly.

Stark rose to his feet on that note. "We may as well stay here for the night," he suggested. "We can build a fire up front, and our backs will be protected."

It was necessary to retrieve the horses and take them back along the rim of the canyon to a point where a descent could be made. Red seemed strangely unsettled when Stark returned for him. The stallion tossed his head and pawed the ground aggressively. Frowning, Stark surveyed the area, but could detect no trace of anything that might have disturbed the animal. Still, the horse's nervousness continued as they made their way to the canyon floor.

In the last minutes of daylight, they again examined the map. The final sketch appeared to be of a towering spire of rock with a yellow sun directly over it.

"I wonder why the sun is in the picture?" Sarah ventured.

"Maybe it shows the time of day," Prudence said thoughtfully. "But why would that matter?"

"I don't know," Stark mused. "But it must matter somehow. The map doesn't show where to go from the pinnacle, which must mean that once you reach it you can see the iron door . . ."

". . . and maybe only when the sun is directly overhead at noon!" Prudence finished for him.

"Yes, that must be it!" Sarah cried excitedly.

From outside the overhang in the gathering shadows, Red snorted loudly. Stark tensed. Something was clearly bothering the horse. He raised his hand to silence the women, then catfooted out into the canyon, revolver in hand. He saw nothing, but even as he stood there the night seemed to fall with bewildering swiftness. The gloom was caught and held by the narrow walls of the canyon.

He scanned the skyline of the canyon rim, and for just an instant he thought he detected movement. Stark's grip tightened on the gun. Surely it was their recent inspection of the Spanish artifacts that made him imagine he saw a head wearing the distinctive outline of a conquistador's helmet etched against the night sky.

Prudence materialized suddenly at his side. "What is it?"

"Nothing," Stark said shortly. "I'll take first watch."

Again the night passed undisturbed. More than once

as he sat his lonely vigil, Stark felt the press of the ghosts of the frustrated dead who seemed to haunt the mountains. Being in this desolate land on a search for dead men's gold was beginning to take its toll on him.

His watch was a tormented period from which he was grateful to escape in sleep when Sarah relieved him. He awoke at dawn to the sounds of Prudence already preparing breakfast.

Sarah roused herself shortly after he did. "I know we'll find the cave today," she said excitedly. "I just know we will!"

The gaiety of her mood remained irritatingly present as they set out. He watched the progress of the sun overhead. By noon he was determined to be atop the stone spire.

It was as he swung Red wide to skirt the site of a recent rockslide that he saw the simple wooden cross set in the ground near the canyon wall. He reined over to it and stared down at the cross atop its mound of earth. The women quickly joined him, and he moved Red aside so they could see the marker.

Sarah gasped as she read the letters burned crudely into the crosspiece: WILLS BANNISTER, R.I.P.

Chapter Nine

Even Sarah's mood was chilled by the discovery of the grave. The gold was momentarily forgotten. "At least it proves Timothy was still alive and made it this far," she insisted stubbornly. "I mean, he had to be the one who buried Bannister."

Stark could only wonder what had killed the old man. Had the strain of the journey been too great for his heart? The landslide beside the grave was of fairly recent origin. Had Bannister fallen victim to it, then been buried almost where he lay?

It was a question they'd have to puzzle out later, for the stone pinnacle which they sought rose majestically at the mouth of a canyon up ahead.

The jagged finger of stone was visible long before they reached it. Stark squinted up at its towering height. Far overhead, level with the summit, a lone eagle soared effortlessly. For an instant the sun caught the white of its head.

They would have to pass through a steep narrow gap at the entrance to the canyon before the walls widened out beyond. Stark signaled a cautious approach. He wasn't sure why, except that his earlier uneasiness at being trapped on the canyon floor had returned with a vengeance.

They proceeded at a walk, and it was a scattering of falling pebbles that alerted him. Far above on the canyon rim he saw the mass of rocks and earth begin to move. Gathering momentum and additional mass as they came, a rain of boulders plummeted upon them, rebounding from the wall, tearing smaller rocks and trees loose in passing.

Turning the horses would take too long. Stark put heels to Red and shouted them forward. The stallion needed no urging. He was already bolting ahead, dragging the burdened packhorse in his wake. Prudence's mare was close beside him. Ahead, Stark had an impression of Sarah's horse stretched out in a dead run, eyes wild with fear, Sarah bent low over the saddle.

Then they were through the narrow neck and out into the open area at the canyon's mouth, clear of the looming walls. The sky stretched wide overhead.

With difficulty Stark hauled Red to a halt. The stallion stood trembling as the women fought to get their horses under control. Stark turned in the saddle to gaze behind them. A last few stones were bouncing to a stop, and a cloud of dust partially obscured the canyon mouth. Despite careful scrutiny, Stark could detect no suspicious movement on the canyon rim.

"Someone started that deliberately," Prudence asserted, coming alongside him.

Stark nodded tersely. There was a slight possibility some animal—perhaps one of the bighorn sheep—could've been responsible. But in his gut, he believed Prudence was right. "I think that's what happened to Wills Bannister as well," he said grimly, recalling the landslide near the grave.

"But who?" Sarah's tone was part plea, part demand. Stark shook his head. "Who knows? I don't think Brockton and his men could've reached the mountains yet. And burying us and the map under a landslide wouldn't be a tactic he'd choose anyway. I suppose it could've been outlaws trying to avoid detection. Or Indians wanting to frighten us away."

None of them wanted to speak the answer which he was sure was in all their minds. *Or the Golden Ones.*

He found the acknowledgement of such a thought disturbing. He struggled to put it away and continue the pursuit of their mission. Timothy Rankin had passed this way recently, and could even now be close at hand. The sooner they located him, the sooner they could leave this dangerous God-forsaken place and return to civilization.

He tilted his head back to gaze up at the summit of the rock spire towering overhead. "We've got to climb it," he admitted grudgingly. "And we've got to hurry."

Prudence shuddered. "Hurrying on a climb like that is a good way to hurry to your grave."

"It can't be helped." He moved Red forward to circle the spire's base, studying it intently.

It was a dozen kinds of foolishness not to investigate the cause of the landslide further, to seek who set it off, if that had actually been the case. But it was already midmorning. They had roughly two hours to reach the top if they were to have a chance of seeing the iron door today. His desire to leave behind the maddening uncertainty of this mission overrode his sense of caution.

On the far side of the pinnacle, so faint and worn they appeared almost a part of the natural surface, Stark detected handholds cut in the rock. Visually tracing their path upward, he saw where natural ledges had been smoothed, crevices widened to make it possible for an active climber to reach the summit.

Though it was clear Sarah wanted to accompany him on the climb, in the end she agreed to wait at the base of the spire with Prudence. Minutes were ticking mercilessly away. In the interest of reaching the summit, it was agreed that Stark would climb alone.

The first handholds lent themselves easily to purchase of hands and feet. Rope coiled over his shoulder, Stetson discarded as an impediment, Stark ascended. He could feel the pull on his muscles as he hauled himself onto a narrow ledge some twenty feet off the ground.

From there he worked his way on up, clinging precariously at times as he sought new purchase. It was all but impossible to discern some of the handholds until they were actually needed. He found himself wondering what redoubtable adventurer had long ago worked out these holds manually. Almost certainly it had been the Spaniards whose ancient progress they now traced. It was not a job he envied them.

At a height of fifty feet, he reached another narrow ledge and rested, panting. He resisted the temptation to peer upward. If he leaned away from the sheer wall at all, he risked losing his balance. He forced himself to concentrate on where he would next put hand and foot.

The ledge angled steeply upward, and he was able to make good progress for a time. Then the grueling, muscle-straining effort began again. Once his foot slipped, sending a small cascade of dirt and pebbles down on the women. Another time he reached to grasp a thick weed protruding from a small crevice, and it came free in his hand. He was forced to jam his fist into the crevice to keep from plummeting to the ground.

The sun rose higher, beating down on him. But Stark forgot the time limits, forgot everything except the barren rock face inches in front of his eyes, the need to fumble for secure holds, to make his fingers grip, his legs drive hard against the abrasive stone.

At the base of a chimney-like crevice he rested and assessed the remainder of the climb. The narrow chimney reached the remaining fifty feet to the summit. But examining its sheer walls, he could find no handholds. The method of ascent, he realized, would have to be with his shoulders against one side and his feet against the other, thereby enabling him to inch his way up. A daunting ordeal for someone whose muscles already ached and trembled with fatigue.

With his shoulders firmly against one wall, Stark braced himself with his feet against the opposite wall and began the tortuous climb. He felt his shoulders scrape across the rough surface as he inched himself upward. Sweat trickled irritatingly into his eyes, and he had to fight the urge to grope frantically with his hands for nonexistent holds.

Three-fourths of the way up, he shifted his foot and the chimney crumbled away beneath it. The world seemed to rotate horribly around him. His body, suddenly relieved of one point of support, revolved in the chimney, and for an eternal agonizing instant he hung suspended there, held by the pressure of his shoulders and one leg, while his other leg flailed reflexively. Then he got his leg back in position, his boot jammed firmly against the far wall again, while terror pounded in his temples and constricted his throat.

There was no real way to rest, however, not with his legs and back braced to take his weight, but he took a moment longer to regain control before he resumed the climb. The last few feet were an agonizing effort, culminated by the wrenching twist necessary to grasp the edge and haul himself out on the pinnacle's barren summit. He sprawled there, panting, shaking with exhaustion.

When at last he was able to move, he rolled over and looked up at the sun. It was directly overhead. The crucial hour was almost upon him. He stood shakily to his feet. The mountain and canyons with their scattered patches of trees stretched away on all sides in a chaotic jumble. Remembering the map, he squinted toward the direction the drawing had indicated.

The sun glared down mercilessly, the heat bouncing back from the stone. Stark drew his shirtsleeve across his forehead and continued to stare. His head began to ache from the intensity of his scrutiny. Then he spotted a darkish rectangle made small by distance, too precise to be natural. It had to be the iron door, set in a weathered cliff face amidst the jumbled terrain.

Shadows, pursued by the sun, were already beginning a relentless march across the cliff face. Within half an hour, he guessed, the door would again be concealed. As he continued to stare, he began to uncoil the rope which he had wrapped around his waist before climbing the chimney. He found a rocky outcropping nearby and secured the rope to it while he continued to memorize landmarks.

The descent to the ground, making use of the rope, was much more rapid than the ascent. A thrusting excitement seemed to charge Stark's muscles, speed his reflexes, heighten his perceptions. Some of it was illusory, he knew, but it felt good to have such exciting news to tell Prudence and Sarah.

Prudence grabbed him and gave him a frantic hug. "Oh, Jim! I was so frightened when you almost fell!"

He couldn't still the smile that split his features. "It didn't do my nerves much good either."

Sarah was fidgeting restlessly behind Prudence. "Did you see anything?" she cried, unable to restrain herself longer.

He nodded. "Yep. I saw what appeared to be the iron door, all right. Of course, we won't know for sure till we take a closer look."

Prudence stared up at him excitedly. "You think you can find it then?"

He nodded again. "That climb scared every other thought out of my head, leaving plenty of room for an indelible etching of the entire area. Let's move out."

The horses sensed their excitement, snorting and tossing their heads against the restraining reins as they rode. With Stark in the lead, they threaded their way amongst the bewildering array of defiles and hills. The iron door, if such it had actually been, was completely lost to sight now. But with every ridge they crested, he found his eyes searching fruitlessly for the dark rectangular shape of it. Realistically, however, he knew it was too soon. He focused on the distinctive peak that served as his target and kept moving forward.

The gully studded with boulders led them upward, the footing for the horses becoming more unsure as the grade increased. Impatiently, Stark pulled Red to a sharp halt as he glimpsed a flicker of movement on the slope to his left. In that same instant he heard a click of sound and something snapped past his head to rattle against the rocks behind him.

He dived off Red on the far side, the butt of the Colt Peacemaker filling his hand even before his feet hit the ground. He triggered the firearm as he landed, using his saddle as a prop. Red stood firm beneath the roar of the gun.

He had aimed almost by instinct at the pile of boulders where he had seen the movement. He shouted now at the women to take cover. He fired again, ducked under Red's neck and raced forward to the protection of a rock outcropping. The boulders were uphill some fifty feet in front of him, but there was ample cover to protect him as he advanced in a series of short fast rushes.

Sunlight flashed off something among the boulders. Stark snapped a shot at it, heard the screeching whine as the slug ricocheted off stone. Then he was among the boulders, caution forgotten in that savage instant. The barrel of the Colt Peacemaker swept across the barren jumble of rocks. No one was there. Their attacker, whoever he had been, had disappeared into the scrub underbrush beyond.

Stark resisted the urge to plunge on in blind pursuit. Following the quarry into his own territory was a greenhorn's move. Reluctantly he returned to where Prudence and Sarah waited near the horses.

Prudence was examining a small object in her hand, and Stark realized that she had retrieved the missile which had been fired at him. Wordlessly she handed it to him. It was a short wooden shaft tipped by a flint point. There were no feathers.

Holding it, even there in the sunlight, Stark felt a cold chill of fear and dread.

"What is it?" Sarah asked nervously.

"A crossbow bolt," Stark answered slowly. His eyes met Prudence's in a fearful union. Neither of them spoke. Words weren't necessary.

A crossbow—favored projectile weapon of the conquistadors.

Chapter Ten

"There it is!" Sarah exclaimed. "I can't believe it!"

They pulled their horses up sharply and stared. Some thirty feet above, set flush in the canyon wall, the massive old door seemed almost a part of the weathered rock surface.

Seeing it now, Stark could well understand how it had remained lost all these years. If they had not been specifically looking for it in this location, they might have missed it altogether. A pathway had been cut into the cliff face to reach the door, Stark saw as they dismounted. Carrying a lantern, they moved cautiously up the path toward their prize.

They halted before the door, the details imprinting themselves in Stark's mind. The door was indeed iron. It was dark with rust and the discoloration of years, and not much over five feet high. An iron frame had been set into the cliff to receive it, the hinges concealed, and a heavy rusted padlock secured it.

Sarah grabbed the padlock and tugged on it impatiently. As she did, Stark noted that the lock, while rusted, didn't seem to be nearly as ancient as the door.

Sarah turned to them in frustration. Stark drew his handgun and shouldered her aside. He didn't want to waste time manipulating an archaic lock mechanism.

The echoes of the shot bounced back and forth between the canyon walls. Stark yanked the shattered padlock loose and dropped it at their feet. Together they put their shoulders against the rough surface of the iron door and strained. Slowly, on protesting hinges, the door swung open beneath the pressure.

They stared into darkness as stale, foul air invaded their nostrils. Sarah started forward, but Prudence caught her arm. "Let's let Jim go first."

The girl nodded, and Stark took the lead after first lighting the lantern. The women pressed close to his back as they ducked through the doorway.

A passageway, obviously widened at some time by human hands, stretched into blackness beyond the glow cast by the lantern. The ceiling was high enough to allow Stark to stand erect. He lifted the lantern and eased forward. He was reminded of the darkened tunnels under the streets of Guthrie and the death which had awaited him there. They moved deeper into the tunnel, the glow of the lantern throwing an uncertain illumination before them along the stone corridor.

After thirty feet, they entered a larger chamber. Stark stopped abruptly, Prudence's gasp sounding in his ear as she gazed, stricken, over his shoulder. He was only dimly aware of her fingers biting into his arm.

The flame of the lantern gave a dull gleam to the brick-shaped items stacked there in profusion. In those first stunned moments, Stark counted a half dozen stacks, three to four feet high and at least that broad at the base. Just as the legend had said, the gold ingots stood waiting there in the darkness to be discovered, exactly as they had for decades.

As his feet carried him stiffly forward, Stark saw the unmistakable white shape on the floor amidst the ingots. A human skull gazed mockingly up at him from a jumble of bones. He didn't look closer. Just as the ancient Indian had described, just as the tales had told, the Spaniards had slain the Indian workers and entombed them here with the product of their labor.

Sarah drifted past them, her face a pale mask in the gloom. She ran her hand distractedly across the nearest ingots. "Timothy was right. The legend was authentic. The treasure is real . . ."

Stark himself reached out and hefted one of the blocky bars. He knew little of gold, but the weight seemed right, and the metal gleamed yellow beneath the light of the lantern. Carefully he returned it to the pile.

Using both hands, Sarah lifted an ingot, as if handling the gold was the only way to substantiate its reality. "Do you think Timothy got to see it too?" she asked in almost a whisper.

Prudence cut her eyes sharply at Stark before answering. "I doubt it, Sarah. That lock hadn't been opened recently. But that doesn't mean we should think the worst."

Before Stark could voice his own reassurances, a whisper of sound—a foot sliding across stone, the creak of metal against leather—touched his ears. In that fragment of an instant, Stark thought of Indian legends, of hidden watchers felt but not seen, of crossbow bolts and something that glinted gold among concealing boulders. He recalled these things, and somehow he knew. So even as he spun to face them at last, he wasn't surprised.

The Golden Ones. Ghosts in ancient battered armor and ragged garments. Six of them, gaunt faces beneath the distinctive helmets, crossbows leveled implacably at the intruders. Stark's hand froze above his gun.

"Good heavens!" Sarah gasped at his shoulder. The ingot dropped forgotten from her hands to thud onto the floor.

The spectral figures were men, not ghosts, Stark realized—men who had entered the tunnel silently behind them and now had him at a dead drop. He would be skewered by the crossbow bolts before he could get off a shot. And crossbows, he remembered from his extensive study of weapons, dispatched their featherless missiles with sufficient force to penetrate armor such as these men wore.

The armor consisted mainly of breastplates and helmets with longswords slung at the waist. The rest of their clothing appeared to be crude leggings, moccasins, and tattered remnants of mismatched attire such as might have been scavenged from their luckless victims over the years.

The men themselves, once the initial shock of confrontation was over, were not nearly so imposing as their bizarre garb made them first appear. None were above medium height and their bearded faces beneath the helmets seemed sallow and gaunt. Their age was hard to determine, but Stark noted the sinewy ridges of muscle on the arms which held the crossbows, the violent competence of their stances. They might be of small stature and perhaps undernourished, but these were still not men to be taken lightly.

Particularly when, as now, he stood helpless beneath the threat of their primitive weaponry.

Their freakish appearance hinted that the legends whispered around campfires all these years, both by Indians and white men alike, were likely all true. In these first few moments of stunned confrontation, Stark was literally at a loss for words.

One of the figures stepped forward slightly. Somewhat stockier than his companions, he was the only one of the six who didn't carry a crossbow. Instead he brandished a naked longsword, elevating its point with a flick of his wrist so that it danced in front of Stark's face. But the man, Stark noted, was careful not to come between the captives and the bows of his associates.

"You have violated the sanctity of el oro del dios," the man said in strangely accented Spanish.

Oro del dios, Stark thought, *gold of the gods.*

He had learned Spanish in his younger years working the big cattle ranches of South Texas, but the armored man's accent and inflections were somewhat strange to him.

Carefully he sought words to form a response in Spanish. "We had no desire to offend you." He kept his hand clear of his gun, but he didn't raise his hands. Rather than submit helplessly, he wanted to leave himself a chance to draw, however small—at least until he was sure which way this situation would break.

"Your sacrilege demands judgment and penalty!" the spokesman jabbed the sword a few inches closer. Stark didn't flinch.

"Are you to be the judge?" he asked boldly. Meek subservience didn't seem to be the role to play.

"That is reserved for Don Luis Mendoza, our captain," the conquistador snapped.

Stark nodded firmly. "We would speak with him then."

The spokesman's face turned ugly. "That is not your choice to make!" he roared, and for a moment Stark thought he would order the bowmen to fire. Instead he gestured sharply with the sword. "I am War Chief Raphael Ortiz Rodriguez. You will surrender your weapons to me immediately."

The war chief title was more appropriate for an Indian tribe, but Stark had no time to pursue the thought.

Rodriguez had extended the sword fully now as if at any instant he might drop into a lunge that would run Stark through. And even if he managed to draw and shoot before the blade drove home, Stark knew he wouldn't escape the bolts from the covering crossbows.

He nodded assent and slowly unfastened his gunbelt, letting it sag to the cave floor. Behind him, Prudence and Sarah followed suit. Disarmed, they were herded out of the treasure vault and back up the passageway into the sunshine.

Once they were outside the tunnel, the massive door was pulled shut. Rodriguez fingered the shattered padlock and glared at them. "You will pay for this! None have ever desecrated the treasure vault as you have."

Seen in the daylight, all of the men bore definite traces of Indian blood. Their beards were sparse, their complexions having a definite copper tint. An idea began to stir in Stark's mind, a partial explanation to the questions clamoring for an answer.

But there was no time to ponder the matter. In front of the bowmen, they were marched back along the canyon floor. Prudence stayed close to Stark's side, and once when their hands brushed she intertwined her fingers with his. Her face was drawn and pale. Sarah was feeling the strain as well. Both her hands clutched at Prudence's other arm. Prudence finally shook her off and slipped an arm around the girl's shoulders. It proved to be a good move. Sarah appeared somewhat calmer after that.

"Can you understand them?" Stark whispered to Prudence.

She nodded. "Mostly. After my mother died, we had a Mexican housekeeper who practically raised me. I grew up speaking Spanish as well as I did English."

"I'm familiar with archaic Spanish such as they're using from helping Timothy translate his research material," Sarah whispered. "I've just never heard it spoken aloud before. Do you think they took Timothy captive like this and are holding him nearby?"

"I have a feeling we'll soon find out," Stark responded.

"Silence!" Rodriguez screeched. "Or you will die!"

The man was on a hair trigger, Stark thought ruefully.

Without ceremony they were hustled inside a narrow crevice that split the canyon wall to the rim some forty feet above. Within a few feet the crevice closed overhead and they were in a cavern passageway. Stark recalled that caves honeycombed parts of these mountains. It was one of the things that had appealed to outlaws over the years. Such caves would also, he realized, make an excellent abode for this clan of displaced conquistadors.

After a few yards, the passageway was lit by small clay oil lamps set in niches at intervals. The walls above the lamps were smudged black, and Stark guessed the smoke must escape through faults in the rock, either natural or devised by their captors.

The passageway widened and they passed the dark mouths of other branches of the cave. They were obviously in a major network of caverns. Faint light glowed far down some of the other corridors, and Stark found himself wondering what took place in those subterranean hallways.

Once, as they passed a divergent artery, a burdened

figure just emerging from it drew up sharply. Stark glimpsed the flat features and dark eyes of a youngish Indian woman before Rodriguez spat guttural words that sent her scuttling back into the darkness. Another piece of the puzzle clicked into place for Stark.

As in the treasure vault, the walls and floor showed definite signs of human workmanship. These caves, Stark realized, might be the original gold mine which produced the ingots. That would explain the work done enlarging and shoring up of the passages. There must also be another exit, he guessed, which would allow the necessary ventilation to clear any smoke from the lamps.

They came at length to a heavy wooden door set in a wall. Rodriguez knocked respectfully, and a voice from within bid them enter. The chamber in which they found themselves held a crude table and chairs and shelves with various items on them. The room's only occupant stood behind the table which apparently served as a kind of desk.

The new man was taller than the others they had seen, and his features were those of a European aristo-crat with little trace of the Indian traits of his compan-ions. His dark hair and beard were streaked with gray, and he appeared slender rather than gaunt, although there was still no excess flesh on him. He was clad in a loose shirt and leggings, and despite his lack of armor a sheathed sword rode at his hip.

"Here are the intruders, Captain," Rodriguez said, stiff with self-importance. He went on briefly to report on their capture, overly emphasizing his own role.

Abruptly, the captain cut him off with a curt gesture. He gazed appraisingly at Stark and the women before he spoke to his subordinate in the same odd Spanish. "You and two of your men may remain here. The rest of you are dismissed."

Three of the bowmen withdrew, and Stark reassessed the odds. He was the target of two crossbows, and Rodriguez had never sheathed his sword. It was still a greenhorn's play to try anything against such odds unless there was no other choice. Besides, he suspected this man, the outpost's leader, possessed the answers to this whole mystery.

He decided to speak first. "My name is James Stark. This is my wife, Prudence, and this is Sarah Walker. We did not realize we had trespassed when we entered the Cave with the Iron Door."

"You have committed a sacrilege by defiling the gold of the gods! The penalty is death!" Rodriguez roared with vehement intensity. His whole face had taken on a dark sinister cast.

Sarah's face registered immediate shock at his pronouncement of the death sentence. She probably feared, and rightly so, that Timothy had received a similar judgment.

Stark wondered if the violent madness Rodriguez exhibited lurked beneath the surface of all who dwelt here. He realized suddenly that their only hope might rest in the man before him.

The captain stood straighter. "I am Don Luis Mendoza, commander of this outpost of Spain. War Chief is right. I am sorry it is my duty to pass this sentence on you, but your own actions have left me no choice."

Stark decided to try reason. "We trespassed in ignorance. We did not know of your duties to protect the gold. Surely you realize no other outposts of your army remain in this land." He half expected his words to spark the fires of madness again.

But Mendoza only shook his head tiredly. "So we have come to believe over the years. But we are bound by the oaths of our forefathers who have passed our holy mission down to us through the generations." He paused and studied them with dark probing eyes. "You are not the first to have told me these things. I know the world beyond our outpost has changed. But what has not changed is the sacred obligation we hold to Spain."

"How old is this outpost?" Prudence asked quietly.

Mendoza seated himself slowly, as if the movements pained him. "Our forefathers set sail from Spain in the year of Our Lord seventeen hundred and fifty under Captain Hernandez Ortega," he said at last. Continuing to speak, his eyes lost focus, as if he recited a narrative he had visualized in his mind many times.

"Captain Ortega was a man of great faith and dedication—faith in the cause of Spain, and dedication to bringing back the riches of the New World for its glory. The voyage lasted a full year, and they endured great hardship. When the ship finally landed, the captain led his men eastward. In their quest for riches, they fought many battles with the pagan peoples of the New World. From captives they learned of a tribe living in a small range of distant mountains where gold was abundant for the taking."

Stark listened as the story unfolded strikingly like the legend he'd heard so many times before.

"After many months and more hardships," Mendoza continued, "the captain and his men reached these mountains and found the tales they had heard were true. They enslaved the tribe and forced them to mine the gold from these very caverns. They even established a smelting operation to refine and purify the gold. The gold bars were stored in another cave which was always guarded, since Ortega believed some of his men might try to steal the gold for themselves. Eventually he sent a squad to retrieve the great iron door from the ship's treasure vault. That door was placed in the entrance of the cave to keep the gold safe until it could be transported to the ship."

Mendoza continued to gaze into the distance as he related how the Indians had ultimately turned on their captors and the madman who led them. In an effort to intimidate the Indians and put an end to the uprising, Ortega had killed the remaining slaves and locked their bodies in with the gold. The effort had only served to further galvanize and enrage the Indians. Most of the Spaniards fled to avoid being slaughtered.

"But Ortega would not leave the gold," the captain related. "He made those who fled vow an oath to return while he and a contingent of his men remained to guard the treasure. They could not conquer the Indians hand to hand, because they were then so outnumbered. But Ortega had his men hide in ambush and strike their foes as opportunity presented itself. Eventually the Indians fought them no more."

Stark could vividly imagine the old Spanish conquistador, by that time almost surely driven insane by his obsession with securing gold and glory for his beloved Spain, leading his men in guerilla warfare against the Indians—haunting them, pursuing them, until at last they had left the caves and their grisly contents to the Golden Ones.

"Many years passed with no sign of anyone returning to relieve them," Mendoza went on. "But Ortega refused to give up his outpost. Some of his men stole Indian women for mates and finally even Ortega himself took a wife. He led his men in vowing a holy oath to dedicate themselves and their children to the cause. And as the children were born, they too were sworn into the cause."

The legacy of a madman, Stark mused. A legacy that

had been perpetuated for many generations as they renewed the vow to uphold the cause—lunacy passed from parents to children and nurtured by a system of indoctrination that began in earliest childhood.

The intermarriage with the Indians explained the racial characteristics of the conquistadors as well as the traces of Indian culture inherent in their clothing and titles. Only the armor, undoubtedly passed down from father to son, remained as a symbol of the madness they had inherited from their ancestors. That plus the gold and the bones of the dead they had slain over the century and a half they had haunted these mountains.

"I am the fifth generation to succeed Ortega," Mendoza announced. "As such, I have inherited the duty to carry on the cause. Many years we have lived in these mountains, adapting these caves where the gold was mined to our use. We have guarded the treasure against all intruders, such as yourselves."

All these years, Stark thought sadly, this small retinue of misguided fanatics had survived—but at what cost? It was not surprising that their features were gaunt, their faces sallow. Living conditions inside the caves couldn't be the best. Nor would food be of abundance. How many of them were there? he wondered.

Slowly the older man pushed himself to his feet. He grimaced once as if in pain, but he stood straight and a stoic resignation began to grow in his eyes. "Because of your own actions, you now must die. It is our duty to execute you to protect the gold."

"I do not believe duty demands the blood of the innocent," Stark said with as much conviction as he could muster. "How can we be judged for transgressing laws of which we had no knowledge?"

"Blasphemer!" The cry came from Rodriguez at his back.

Stark forced himself not to turn. He continued to look directly at Mendoza. "We at least deserve the right to a trial."

"Enough!" Rodriguez cut him off sharply. "When you enter a foreign land you are subject to the laws of that land. Our laws demand your execution!"

"War Chief is right," Mendoza agreed, almost reluctantly it seemed. "It has always been so. You have defiled the gold and spoken blasphemy before us all."

Stark's heart sank. The rational side of the man was being displaced by the years of fanatical indoctrination and a warrior's sense of duty, perhaps sparked by Rodriguez's hysterical interjections into the conversation.

There was an abrupt knock at the wooden door. Rodriguez jerked it open to reveal one of their original captors. The soldier approached the table and deferentially leaned close to consult with the captain.

Stark watched as the old man's expression changed to one of fierce dread, tinged by a flicker of fear. Then a new resolve settled over his features and he straightened even further.

"Your execution must be postponed, it seems," he proclaimed. "War Chief will be otherwise occupied for a while. A large party of men has entered the mountains, more than we have ever dealt with. They all appear to be fighting men. I am sure they are seeking the gold."

Chapter Eleven

Stark felt a rush of hope. He continued to address Mendoza. "I know these men," he said quietly. "You are right. They are after the gold. But they are my enemies more than yours. Free me, and I will help you fight them."

"We will fight them alone!" Rodriguez cried. "And we will win! We have always defeated our enemies unaided."

Stark saw the doubt and fear on the messenger's face. The new conquistador clearly wasn't convinced. "But War Chief, there are a great number of them this time. More than even our ancestors encountered. And our fathers were many, while we are few."

"Silence!" Rodriguez bellowed. "You speak treason! Our victory is assured! We guard the gold for the gods. The gods will see that we win a victory!"

Mendoza had been studying the newcomer as well. He held up a hand to silence all discussion. "Your execution must be postponed!" he repeated. "War Chief, imprison them. We must assess the situation and make plans for battle. I will go myself and view these new intruders."

Rodriguez seemed on the verge of yet another venomous outburst, but he managed to control himself as he turned angrily away. Stark had one last glimpse of his fiery demented gaze as he, Prudence, and Sarah were led away.

It was no wonder, Stark thought, that for decades these mountains had been considered cursed and haunted by Indians and white men alike. And no wonder he had felt they were the subject of invisible scrutiny since they had entered the area. Mendoza's conquistadors must have been stalking them for days. At least twice, by landslide and crossbow, they had tried to kill them.

As they had killed Wills Bannister. And almost certainly, Stark feared now, as they had killed Timothy Rankin.

These thoughts spun numbly in Stark's mind as he and the women were escorted down other dim passages. At last they halted before an opening in the wall covered by a rough metal gridwork of bars. This cell door was secured by an ancient padlock similar to the one on the treasure vault. Rodriguez unbolted the door, and they were unceremoniously pushed inside.

The only light in their prison was cast by the small oil lamps in the passageway outside. As the grid was once again secured, something stirred in the gloom and a hoarse voice gave a muffled exclamation. Stark saw Sarah tense. She gasped as a bearded scarecrow of a figure moved toward them out of the darkness.

"Timothy!" she cried, rushing into his welcoming arms with such force that she almost bowled him over.

Stark and Prudence could see little of their fellow prisoner until at last Sarah disentangled herself and made breathless introductions. The young professor was tall, his natural slender build only accentuated by what had obviously been a period of severe hardship. His clothes were torn, and a stubbly unkempt beard obscured the lower part of his face. But his hand, when he gripped Stark's, had a wiry strength to it.

Prudence's face was wreathed in a smile that said clearly all the danger and hardship had been worth it to witness this moment. She gave Sarah a joyful hug as the two young people told each other of their individual journeys in breathless rushes.

Leaving them to their confused explanations, Stark prowled the cell in which they had been imprisoned. The chamber was obviously the beginning of a mining excavation which, for whatever reason, had been halted in its early stages. The rough stone walls enclosed an area some twenty feet square. The ceiling was of uneven height. The only exit was the grid through which they had entered.

"You can forget getting out unless they let us out." Timothy Rankin might have been reading Stark's mind. "I've been over every inch of these walls." Though he and Sarah still clung together almost frantically, he had been watching Stark's inspection.

Stark turned his attention to the man. "How long have you been here?"

"Who knows?" Rankin flung up both hands jerkily. "All my life it seems . . ." Abruptly he swayed. Prudence reached for him, but Sarah was already at his side, helping him to be seated on a pallet of dried grass in the corner. She dropped to her knees beside him and remained there attentively while Stark and Prudence sank to a similar pallet facing the pair.

"Sorry," Rankin apologized, running a hand through

his tangled hair. "Too much excitement, I guess. It's not every day I have visitors. What's the date anyway?"

Stark told him.

Rankin shook his head. "It seems longer. But I guess six months is long enough." He grinned at Sarah's sharply indrawn breath. "It's all right, sweetheart, I've gotten by. I've mentally composed most of my treatise on the lifestyle of the Spanish conquistadors in the New World. Lord knows I've had ample opportunity to observe it first hand." His words were tinged with bitterness. "Maybe someday I'll get the chance to write it down."

"Why did they allow you to live in the first place?" Prudence asked curiously.

"When they captured me they found some of my texts with drawings of the old Spanish conquistadors. They were so intrigued, particularly Mendoza, that they kept me alive."

"Do they ever let you out?" Stark asked.

Rankin shook his head. "Not anymore. They used to, but they haven't in a long time. Mendoza used to question me about my work and my books. I'd never spoken Spanish before, but I was very familiar with it in the written form. So I was able to pick it up quickly enough, and managed to satisfy him for a while. But we never did really communicate. They're so isolated here, the world I described—the world we come from—is totally irrelevant to them. Mendoza quickly lost interest in what I had to say. Now, for all I know, he's completely forgotten about me."

"Well, I'm just grateful you're alive," Sarah said excitedly. "I can't believe you got away from Brockton and actually made it to the canyon with no trouble."

Rankin laughed ruefully. "Well, believe it or not, getting away from Brockton was the easy part. I was able to string him along and pretend to be interested in his offer of a partnership. I had no intentions of letting him see the map, however. I figured I'd be killed as soon as he got his hands on it. He hardly seemed trustworthy."

Stark snorted. "That's an understatement if ever there was one. The man's an out and out criminal."

Rankin nodded. "I figured as much. Bannister didn't trust him either. We managed to slip out of White City late one night with a copy of the map, and actually made it here to the mountains without incident. Between the map and Bannister's memory of the earlier expedition, we were able to make rapid progress . . . until he was killed, that is . . ."

The young man's voice trailed off hopelessly, and Sarah again reached for his hand.

Timothy smiled weakly. "At the time, I didn't realize these maniacs had started the landslide. I thought it was fate. So I buried him and kept going. I actually saw that blamed iron door, but that's as close as I got. Rodriguez and his crew popped up out of nowhere and were ready to execute me then and there when one of them found my books. Even Rodriguez got excited over the pictures, and he's the craziest one of the lot."

"How many of them are there in all?" Stark wanted to know.

"Twelve men including Mendoza, and probably a half dozen women. There are no children that I've seen. They really have a fascinating culture. They've kept some of the trappings of the conquistadors, but they've also adopted the lifestyle of the Indians in many ways. That's how they've managed to survive this long."

Stark cut off the lecture. "Are there any regular guards?"

"No, no guards at all, really. There's no need, since

we can't get out of the cell without their help." He flung an evil glare at the grating. "They bring food and water once a day, and Rodriguez comes by to harass me every so often. That would be almost entertaining, if the man weren't so dangerous. I have the feeling that at any moment something might snap in his twisted mind; then there's no telling what he will do."

Remembering the maniacal demeanor of the war chief, Stark couldn't help but agree with Rankin's assessment. "You said he's the worst of them?"

Rankin nodded. "But they're all a little bit mad, you know. However, Rodriguez seems the most overtly dangerous. Even in his saner moments, he's fanatically jealous of Mendoza."

Sarah shifted about on the straw until she was closer to her fiance, then tucked her legs under her and leaned her head briefly against his shoulder. Stark glanced at Prudence and saw her smile warmly at the sight of the two of them together.

Stark couldn't bring himself to share his wife's joy at the reunion. Rankin had held up amazingly well under the conditions, but his words hardly boded well for the future. Would the four of them still be here when another six months had passed?

Or would they be dead at the hands of the insane war chief?

Wordlessly he rose and resumed his inspection of the cell. Rankin and Sarah continued to talk in a low voice with Prudence. Stark heard his own name mentioned frequently, and knew his part in the mission was being discussed. He ignored them, and continued his examination of their prison.

He soon decided Rankin was right. There was no way out of the chamber except through the barred entrance.

He was standing, hands on his hips staring at it, when without warning a helmeted figure was suddenly silhouetted against the opening. He recognized the evil sneering features of War Chief Rodriguez. Rankin and the women fell abruptly silent.

"You will all die!" Rodriguez hissed, resting his gaze finally on Rankin. "Even you, whom our captain has spared in the past. I will see to it. Our captain will listen to me now that you have led others to the treasure. You should perish by fire and sword for your desecration and blasphemy."

He glanced about as if checking for listeners. "And if our captain is too weak to carry out his duties, then I will do it myself. The captain is old and weak. Already the other men look to me for leadership. Me, War Chief Rodriguez!"

Stark decided to bait him. "You lie. You have no say in this matter."

Rodriguez's face twisted in fury until it seemed an inhuman gargoyle peered in at them. With a wordless sound of rage, he hauled his sword free and shoved it through the bars at Stark's face. Stark sidestepped slightly and resisted the urge to grab the blade in his naked hands.

Rodriguez left the sword in front of him an instant too long, doing some baiting of his own, Stark guessed. Then gradually his features relaxed. "You are clever, but I have seen through your trickery. I could even give you this sword, and it would not benefit you. It would merely hasten your death, as then I could summon all our warriors to kill you!"

Stark nodded. "True, but only if Captain Mendoza allowed it."

For just an instant the bestial rage flashed across his face again, then disappeared. "Perhaps the captain will not always be in command here. You would do well to keep that in mind."

With that parting threat he was gone, almost like a phantom. Stark listened as the brush of his moccasins on stone faded away. Despite himself, Stark found he'd been holding his breath. The madness of this place was truly intimidating.

"Watch it with him," Rankin warned in a strained voice. "He's too dangerous to toy with."

Stark resented the reprimand. "We've got to get out of here some way," he shot back. "He's so sure of himself, he'll get careless at some point. Then I'll be able to get hold of him instead of the sword, and I'm betting he keeps a key to this cell on him somewhere. He'd want to be able to get at us without asking permission of anyone else."

Prudence rose and came to stand close beside him. She laid a restraining hand lightly on his arm. He pulled her against him, struggling to project a calm he didn't feel.

Sarah looked up at them from where she sat with tears in her eyes. "This is all so crazy! These poor people hiding in these holes like rats! And all because of that gold. It's so seductive. I mean, it was even affecting me. When I held that gold bar in my hands—"

Timothy caught her by the shoulders and jerked her around to face him. "You saw the gold? It really exists?"

Sarah nodded dejectedly. "But so what? What does it get us in here?"

Rankin gave a groan. "You're right. It's not worth anything in here. Old Wills spent his life dreaming about that gold and planning ways to come back for it. When he saw I had a map he almost collapsed right then. I didn't think he was strong enough to make the trip. He'd been drinking heavily for years. I was surprised he was still alive. But the dream of the gold kept him going. All it bought him in the end, though, was death under a pile of rocks."

The young man shook his head sadly. "I got him loose while he was still alive. He kept talking about the gold right up until he died. By then I knew perfectly how he felt. I went into this treasure hunt thinking it would help advance my career. If I could verify the legend and prove the Spaniards had really mined gold here, it would establish me as the top authority in the country, give me recognition over older men who had been researching the matter for years. It seemed like the perfect climax to my career."

Rankin clearly regretted the facts he was revealing about his motives, but he kept talking resolutely. "But after I met Wills and heard him describe the gold, I began thinking there was nothing wrong with wanting both professional success *and* riches. I told myself we needed the money for your sake, Sarah. But by the time I got here to the mountains, I think maybe the gold had taken precedence over everything else . . ."

"How did Douglas Brockton get involved?" Prudence asked. Stark was grateful she'd found a way to lead Rankin out of the useless introspection.

"I'm really not sure how he found out about my efforts. He showed up shortly after I contacted the son of the treasure hunter who'd been on that earlier expedition. He implied he had information concerning the location of the cave. I believed he was legitimate at first. The man's quite convincing at times—even charming, when he wants to be."

"Yeah, I've experienced his *charm* first hand," Stark said sarcastically. "You're just lucky he didn't get around to using physical means to induce you to let him in on the deal."

"You mean that sleazy gunfighter and that big gorilla of a brawler on his payroll? Bannister and I didn't stick around long after they came on the scene. We figured he brought them in to coerce us into cooperating with him. We didn't give him the chance. If I'd known he would then go after Sarah, I might have done things differently. But at the time, sneaking out of town seemed the best course of action."

"It *was* the best course," Prudence asserted. "It probably saved your life."

Timothy dropped his head to his hands. "Not that my life is worth all that much. Look how I've squandered it so far—and not only my life, but all of yours as well."

"We're not dead yet," Stark growled. "In fact, the mission's pretty much on track so far. We found you, didn't we?"

"In a way, I wish you hadn't," Rankin moaned. "I wish you'd just persuaded Sarah to go back home where she would be safe."

"No one could've persuaded me to do that," Sarah insisted.

"I can't believe you still feel that way," he said. "I acted like a total fool, and look where it got me."

Stark didn't speak this time. They were right back to the point he'd tried to make repeatedly with Sarah throughout this trip. How many lives had this lost cache claimed over the years? Beginning with Captain Ortega and his demented dream passed down through the generations of deluded followers. Reaching out to ensnare those who sought after the gold only to find death at the hands of the Golden Ones. Timothy and Sarah, both caught up in the feverish quest for the treasure. And now even Prudence and himself, facing death due to their desire to protect Sarah and reunite her with her lost love.

He shook his head vigorously, as if he needed a physical act to dislodge the feelings of dread and doom that assailed him. Perhaps the worst curse of the gold was the way it stole optimism and hope from all who encountered it.

"We're not dead yet," he growled again, this time more for his own benefit than that of the others.

Chapter Twelve

Don Luis Mendoza stood erect behind his table desk as they were ushered into his quarters. The captain's face seemed more gaunt and haggard than when they had first seen him the previous afternoon, Stark thought. He was extremely aware of the evil presence of Rodriguez close behind them as he and the others halted in front of the desk.

They had been brought from the dungeon following a restless night's sleep that had produced only aching joints and muscles, rather than recovery from the previous day's harrowing events. It was small consolation to Stark that Mendoza appeared to have been wrestling with demons of his own during the hours of the night.

But the old conquistador stood ramrod straight as they were brought before him. Over the protests of Rodriguez, he ordered the bowmen to wait outside the closed door. Curtly, he told the war chief that he might remain in the room.

Angrily, Rodriguez went to stand guard on one side of the door. Mendoza remained motionless, staring at Stark with unblinking intensity until Prudence shifted uncomfortably. As if the movement broke the spell which had held him, Mendoza shook his head sharply. Turning he began to pace back and forth.

"I have just returned from viewing the war party that has entered our mountains. Since they do not know the terrain as we do, they still remain perhaps two days' ride away. But they are coming toward us with certainty. I fear that we will have to confront them eventually to keep them from finding the gold . . . and our outpost here."

Stark was finding the archaic Spanish increasingly easier to understand. "How many of them are there?" he asked, imitating the inflection as closely as he could.

"In your numbers, twenty-five, perhaps more. It was dark when we reached their camp. We counted the men around the campfires, and estimated the guards."

"So you are outnumbered two to one," Stark ventured.

"How do you know how many there are of us?" Rodriguez spat.

"I told him," Timothy spoke up calmly. "I have had much time to observe your outpost."

Rodriguez turned on him threateningly. "Yes, you have had *too* much time. It should not have been so." He cast a disparaging glance at Mendoza. "You should have been executed long ago."

"Silence!" Mendoza ordered. "We must deal with the future, not the past." He turned to another table behind him, and peeled back a tapestry to reveal the array of weapons they'd confiscated from Stark and the women.

"The invaders are heavily armed," he continued. He picked up one of the rifles. "They have many such pieces as these."

"I expect they do," Stark said. "Such firearms are

common nowadays. Surely you've encountered men armed with them before this time."

"We have seen them many times," Rodriguez hissed venomously. "But those carrying them never had a chance to fire them. With the help of the gods we killed them and destroyed their weapons before they had a chance to use them against us."

"Picking off a solitary horseman with a crossbow or burying a rider under a landslide won't work this time," Stark said calmly. "There are simply too many of them. This time it will mean a serious all out battle."

"Must we listen to this blasphemy?" Rodriguez snarled.

Mendoza ignored him and continued to address Stark. "You said these men were more your enemies than ours. How do you know them?"

"They have tried to kill all of us before, even the young man you have held captive all these months. They knew we had a map to lead us to the Cave with the Iron Door, and they wanted this map."

"See! It is their fault these men have come," Rodriguez continued his tirade. "They should die, then we will take care of the others."

Mendoza sighed tiredly. "I am not sure we can."

Rodriguez strode forward. "Now even you speak blasphemy! We must not relinquish this holy trust given to us by the gods!"

"By the gods?" Stark inserted. "Or by a madman dead for a hundred years?"

"The God I worship," Prudence said tentatively, "is more concerned about the lives and welfare of His people than He is about riches and gold."

Stark couldn't see Rodriguez's face, but he saw the violent tension spasm through the man's body.

"So the women also join in the sacrilege! You must silence them all, Captain. We cannot be swayed from our sacred duties. We must remain true to our heritage!"

The weariness and fatigue grew more pronounced on Mendoza's lined face. "I have begun to question many things about our heritage, War Chief. Each year we grow fewer in number and our lifespans are shorter. Now, for the first time, there are no children to carry on our mission. Unless we steal children from the Indians and raise them up in our traditions, there will be no outpost here when the last of us are dead. Then what will happen to the gold for which you say we should sacrifice our very lives?"

"You forget your sacred charge, Captain." His words were a barely audible whisper.

Mendoza shook his head sadly. "I do not think so. Perhaps I am just now becoming aware of my responsibilities as your leader. Is it my sacred charge to continue to advance the policies of a man long dead, policies that can only end in death for us all?"

Rodriguez reeled back as if struck. His hand gripped his sword hilt and the weapon slid half free of its sheath. Stark tensed to spring, but then Rodriguez shoved the sword back into its scabbard and stalked wordlessly from the room. Stark had one glimpse of the war chief's face. He fervently wished he hadn't.

Mendoza gazed sorrowfully after his second in command. Gone, Stark realized, was all trace of the blind obedience to duty that had lurked in Mendoza on their first meeting. He prayed the man would continue to fight his way free of the madness.

Stark nodded toward the door through which Rodriguez had passed. "That one is your enemy."

"I know." Mendoza sighed. "One day he will turn on

me, even if it means the destruction of our outpost. But it is beyond me to have him put to death."

Tiredly he sank into his chair, motioning them onto the crude wooden benches in front of the desk. Briefly the old conquistador pressed a hand to his chest and a pained expression crossed his face. "But all he may need to do is wait. My health is not good. I have pains in my chest of late and at times my head aches as if my skull is going to split. And now I question what we do here. When I was younger it seemed important to protect the gold, to kill those who came into these mountains seeking it. But even as we sit here, I do not know why I should kill you, though Rodriguez would tell me it is the will of the gods."

Stark sensed the man was in a supreme struggle. He almost feared to speak. Anything he said might be the wrong thing, and push the man back into the dark evil world he was struggling so hard at the moment to leave behind.

Mendoza abruptly shifted his eyes to the array of guns spread out on the table. "You are good with these weapons?"

"The best," Stark said without blinking. Here, at last, was a question he could answer without fear.

"And you say you would use them to help us defeat those of your own kind? I have trouble believing this."

Stark again met the man's gaze. "Those men are enemies of all people. They have broken many laws in my world. I fight such men as these all the time and bring them to justice."

"Justice!" Mendoza snorted. "Justice is decided by the strong and imposed on the weak—just as our ancestors imposed their will on the Indians who mined the gold for them."

"Not in our culture," Prudence joined in the conversation. "We have a system of laws, put in place by a majority of the people to govern and protect all citizens—even the weak. It is called a democracy."

Mendoza stared from Stark to Prudence incredulously. "This land, this culture sounds . . . unreal to me."

"Oh, it's very real," Prudence said evenly. "And though you have never availed yourself of the benefits of living here, it is your country too. You are under the protection of its laws."

"But should I avail myself of the protection of its laws, I would also be under their condemnation and subject to their judgment . . ."

Stark held his breath. Prudence had led the old man one step too far. If he grasped any of what she'd said, he knew well he was guilty of murder many times over in ordering the deaths of the treasure seekers who had ventured into these mountains in the past.

The confusion and despair were clearly visible on Mendoza's face. He pressed his fingers to his head for a long moment, then rose to his feet. "You have given me much to think about. I must take time to consider all the aspects of the situation, and to confer with my men."

He walked over to the door and summoned the two guards inside. "I will ask the guards to show you to a room down this passage where you can wait. I will call you when something is decided."

The room where they were escorted was another stone chamber. The only difference Stark could see was that it was closed off by a heavy wooden door instead of the locked metal grate. Rankin and the women sank silently onto crude wooden bunks, but impatience grated on Stark's nerves as he paced restlessly about.

Finally, he sank down beside Prudence to wait hopelessly as the hours dragged past.

By now, it had to be near dusk. Another day had passed.

Stark's sleep that night was more of a collapse into exhausted unconsciousness than true slumber. His dreams were of the kind best left forgotten, and he awoke to a leaden eagerness to get on with a life that had been halted at the whim of insanity run amuck.

They were watered and fed—a thin gruel that was tasteless and unsatisfying. Stark had barely finished his portion when a helmeted guard opened the door. He indicated Stark. "The captain wishes to see you." He sounded almost puzzled.

Stark accompanied the man, wondering at his odd attitude. The conquistador walked just a little ahead of him and did not carry a primed crossbow, as had been the case of the guards he had thus far encountered. It was almost as if the man considered himself a guide. The idea stunned Stark, and the possibility of overcoming his companion only vaguely occurred to him.

There was a definite tension vibrating in the passages of the outpost. Stark sensed it in the quickness of his companion's movements, in the darting glances of his eyes. Once, they passed two other conquistadors—men Stark had never seen—and the pair's greetings to his guard were terse, their expressions sullen. They looked darkly at Stark and then strode on.

Shortly, the guard brought him to Mendoza's door. At the man's respectful knock, Mendoza's voice bid them enter. The guard was dismissed, although not without a curious backward glance. Then Stark faced the captain alone.

Mendoza still looked worn and tired, but there was a

subtle resignation on his features and in his stance. He regarded Stark gaugingly before he spoke. "I trust your quarters were more adequate."

Stark nodded. "Anything beats being locked in a dungeon."

"I'm sorry for the delay, but it was necessary to prepare and plan. The group of armed men are moving ever closer. My warriors all agreed that we have no chance against a band of their number. Yet they are still reluctant to allow you to lead the attempt to defeat the strangers."

"That's understandable." Stark hoped he knew where the conversation was headed. He breathed a simultaneous sigh of relief and prayer of gratitude. "What about you? Are you reluctant as well?"

"Perhaps not as much," Mendoza said with surprising candor. "I have known you were different from the first. You have about you the air of a warrior."

Stark blinked. For someone who had led such an isolated existence, Mendoza showed exceptional perception. "And this is what you seek?"

Mendoza's frankness continued. "It is not necessarily what I seek, but it is what I need at this time. I fear I must ask your advice on matters of war."

Stark had only a moment to reflect on the miracle which had transformed him from prisoner under sentence of death to adviser and confidant of his captor. He became aware of a growing stress in Mendoza's eyes and features. "What has happened?"

"War Chief Rodriguez has disappeared."

Chapter Thirteen

From where he crouched with his armored companion in scrub brush well above a rocky defile, Stark had a clear view of the long column of men riding in pairs below them.

Mendoza had been right. They were all fighting men—hired guns and hardcases selling their guns and their souls to the highest bidder. And even from this distance, there was no mistaking the identity of their leader. Douglas Brockton sat his big bay with the casual arrogance which was so much a part of his nature. There was no outward evidence of the gunshot wound Stark had inflicted.

Stark still found it hard to believe the man had been able to organize a small army and reach the mountains this soon. It bespoke not only an iron physical conditioning, but also a brutal determination.

Watching the man now from concealment, recalling the violence of which he was capable, Stark felt a staggering dread at the task that lay before him and the group of poorly trained and equipped conquistadors.

Riding beside his master, slouched insolently in the

saddle, was the slender figure of the gunfighter Milo Hawk. He was plainly acting as Brockton's lieutenant. Brockton had brought his best men on this journey.

The other members of the party were of the ilk Stark had constantly dealt with since becoming involved with Brockton. A few at a time, they were easily defeated. But now their sheer numbers were daunting.

Stark glanced at his companion, a young man named Jorge Escobar, clad now in his full armor, sword and dagger at his side, crossbow slung across his back. Stark had a brief instance of almost disbelief that he crouched here allied with this throwback to an ancient age of exploration and conquest.

As Escobar returned his glance, it was evident he regarded Stark with a certain reverence and awe. And certainly, Stark thought, the rapid transformation in this man's hitherto closed world must seem incredible to him. A condemned prisoner, an intruder from the outside world, had been granted power little short of Mendoza's own. Only the complete and hereditary authority which Mendoza wielded over his men had enabled him to enforce his orders concerning Stark and his companions.

Recalling his earlier conversation with the captain, Stark himself felt a little awed by the events. When he'd had his early morning meeting with Mendoza, he had asked for a complete update on the situation.

Mendoza had complied, giving great details about the location and progress of Brockton's party. "They do not come to the treasure cave as directly as you and your friends did, but they are getting nearer nonetheless. Do they have a map also?"

"I don't believe so. I think they have merely come into the mountains hoping to overtake me and the women, and through us to locate the Cave with the Iron

Door. The leader is a very greedy and dangerous man. Did your scouts take any action against them?"

"No. Their numbers are too great. Often on small groups of invaders, my men will act. But during my command of the outpost, we have not encountered a group so large."

And the Spanish outpost might well have not survived if they had, Stark thought. But he didn't voice the thought aloud. "How close by are they?"

"For one who knows the trails, a few hours travel from here."

Stark considered the information. It was always possible that Brockton had found a tracker talented enough to have actually trailed him here, but the odds were against it. Likely the men would merely continue to press into the mountains in hopes of encountering him, just as he'd told Mendoza. "And you say they're headed in this direction?"

"Only in a general fashion. I have instructed the scouts to keep careful track of their progress and report in often."

Stark nodded. He didn't know how much leeway his new position as adviser afforded him. "Since you and your men don't speak their language and I do, I would like to see the party of men myself," he said carefully. "I might be able to overhear their battle plan."

Mendoza accepted his request without apparent qualm. "One of my men can take you immediately."

Stark hid his relief. "It may be that we can avoid contact with them altogether. They do not know the location of the cave, and it is unlikely that they will happen upon it by accident."

Even as he spoke, however, Stark had an alarming image of Brockton's men spreading out over the mountainous terrain in a relentless search for the elusive iron door. It was not a pleasant thought. Given Brockton's fanatical commitment to locate the treasure, a confrontation between his men and the conquistadors seemed almost inevitable. Despite his own words, he feared it was entirely possible that a systematic organized search would, over time, lead to the discovery of the treasure cave.

"I do not wish to fight these men," Mendoza said firmly. "But I fear that if they find us or the gold, it will mean war."

Stark nodded in agreement. Given the nature of Brockton and his men, the conquistadors would most certainly be forced into a fight, if only in self-defense. "What about Rodriguez?" he asked to change the subject.

"As I told you, he has disappeared. No one has seen him since he left my office in anger. He cannot be found."

"You have searched the entire compound?"

"In a limited way. But I must also use men to keep track of the intruders and relay information of their progress."

Stark nodded again. "I understand. Nevertheless, while I am gone, a guard should be placed over my companions."

Mendoza pondered Stark's concern. "I will see to their safety," he agreed. "Rodriguez is unpredictable, and he will be enraged when he learns I have freed you and forbidden a confrontation with the intruders. I am concerned he might initiate such action himself to force me to act as he thinks I should."

The prospect of that happening was indeed within the realm of possibility, Stark had to acknowledge, knowing the evil war chief.

Was Rodriguez even now lurking in the darkness of

some forgotten passage deep in the labyrinth, waiting to strike down Mendoza and seize control of the outpost? Or plotting some evil against Rankin, Prudence, and Sarah?

Mendoza might have read his thoughts. "I will see that your wife and the others are kept safe. And I will provide you with a guide immediately."

"First I must speak to my wife," Stark insisted. "And I want the guns you took from us returned." A final test. Stark knew he was pressing his luck, but he refused to leave Prudence and the others helpless.

Mendoza pondered again, but in the end gave a reluctant nod. "I suppose if I am to trust you, I must go all the way. You may return to your friends, but I think it best if you hurry."

Stark nodded. An urgency was already gnawing at him to get moving and assess the danger Brockton and his war party posed. He crossed to the table where his arms and those of his companions were still spread out as if on display. He quickly strapped on the Colt Peacemaker, and gathered up the handguns to return to Prudence and Sarah. The extra gun from his saddlebags he took along to give to Rankin. Stark had no idea how experienced the man was as a gunhand, but he needed to be armed.

Prudence rushed into his arms when he entered the room where they had spent the night. He held her tightly, acutely aware of how precious this woman had become to him. He answered her questions quickly, while Timothy and Sarah looked on.

Finally he cut her off. "Rodriguez has disappeared," he said tensely as he passed out their guns, "and Mendoza has asked my advice about how to handle Brockton and his men. If possible, we're hoping to avoid a confrontation with such a large war party."

Prudence looked relieved. "So we got through to Mendoza after all. Perhaps we can get out of here without fighting Brockton and his men. They don't have a map. Surely they won't be able to find the cave. And after they leave, we can just go home."

"Let's pray toward that end, anyway," Stark said solemnly. "I'll know better after I have a look."

Prudence caught his hand. "Be careful."

He nodded and left the room. A single guard— Mendoza's promised protection—stood outside the door in the passage. The captain's forces were being spread thin by this series of crises.

The cross-country journey with the young conquistador was an experience for which Stark, with all his skill at tracking and woodcraft, was ill prepared. It was no wonder these people had managed to exist undetected here in these mountains for so long.

Escobar led him through narrow passes, around steep ridges, and up hidden draws, staying always to the cover of rocks or vegetation, never skylining himself or his charge. And despite all the precautions, they still made excellent time. Stark wasn't surprised that this young man's forefathers had been able to fight the Indians native to these hills to a humiliating defeat using such guerrilla tactics. And of necessity as their numbers had dwindled, their expertise at concealment and combat in this terrain had only heightened over the decades.

Now, watching the riders passing below, Stark realized that he, Prudence, and Sarah had been under similar scrutiny since they had reached the vicinity of the cave. He knew there must be at least one more of Mendoza's men pacing Brockton's forces from concealment. But even being aware of that fact, he couldn't detect the other man's location.

Brockton's voice, raised to be heard at the end of the column of riders, ordered a halt. As the men dismounted, Stark saw Brockton confer briefly with Hawk. Stark's hand tightened on the shotgun. With two shots he could remove the war party's leadership and negate most of the threat it offered. Then slowly he forced himself to relax.

With no certainty that the intruders would ever even find the cave, it didn't appear to be the wisest course of action.

Watching him, Escobar had silently unlimbered his crossbow. Stark shook his head slightly. The young man frowned, but didn't question the decision. Brockton and Hawk were still talking. Stark decided it would be a perfect opportunity to try and gain some knowledge of their plans.

With gestures, Stark communicated his desire to Escobar. The young conquistador smiled, as if pleased to be able to demonstrate his abilities. He took the lead, and they began to work their way down through the rocks and brush toward Brockton. It was a painstaking process of crouching and crawling on hands and knees and belly, with frequent pauses to get their bearings.

In only moments, however, they eased into a brush-choked draw and worked their way up to within some twenty feet of the spot at the head of the column where Brockton and Hawk stood.

From where he lay, hardly daring to breathe, Stark could see that the journey, coupled with the bullet wound, had left its mark on Brockton after all. The handsome face was drawn and marred by new lines. He moved stiffly, and Stark guessed that it was for Brockton's own comfort, as much as for that of the men, that he had ordered a rest period.

For his part, Milo Hawk looked as lean and deadly as ever. He had discarded his tailored suit, but the holstered .45 still clung to his hip in its unadorned holster like it was a part of him. The harsh lines and planes of his face betrayed no emotion as he listened to his employer speak.

"These blasted mountains are a maze!" Brockton spat in disgust. "There's no way we'll ever find that cave at this rate." He lifted his forearm and drew it across his brow to wipe away the sweat. He winced as he did so, as if the movement brought him pain.

"We could split the boys up into pairs," Hawk suggested. "Cover more ground that way."

Brockton scowled darkly. "I don't like the idea. I know Stark is in these hills somewhere. If we split up we'd only make it easier for him to pick us off one by one, and he's just the man who could do it. You said yourself you'd heard how he used to hunt outlaws in these parts back when he was a bounty hunter."

Brockton paused and looked about him suspiciously. "Besides, there are simply too many stories about people going into these mountains and never coming out again. There's strength in numbers, and for now we'll just keep operating like we have been."

"I hope Stark *is* here." Hawk's voice was soft, and his palm brushed caressingly over the butt of his revolver. "And I hope I get a chance at him."

"Well, if you do get a chance, kill him and be done with it," Brockton said sourly. "Don't go giving him a chance at you. That's an amateur's move. Remember, I've seen him in action." He rubbed his injured shoulder for emphasis. "The man's good with a gun."

"I'm faster," Hawk said simply.

"You better be smarter too," Brockton said shrewdly.

"That's what I'm paying you to be. Just remember what I said."

Hawk turned away wordlessly, his hand still stroking the .45. Abruptly he wheeled about to gaze down the draw where Stark and Escobar lay prone in the grass.

"What's wrong?" Brockton demanded.

"We're being watched," Hawk said slowly. "I can feel it."

Brockton didn't question the man's pronouncement. His eyes raked over the surrounding ridges while Hawk scanned the brush and rocks around them.

Stark held his breath. Beside him, he knew Escobar was doing the same. He forced his mind into emptiness, his body into total stillness. He literally felt Hawk's gaze touch him and pause. If the gunman had indeed spotted them, they were lost. He might be able to take Hawk in the first moment of surprise, provided Escobar could account for Brockton. But after that, the guns of the remaining men would cut them both down. Ever so slowly he tensed his right arm in preparation for drawing his gun. Possibly for the last time . . .

Then Hawk's eyes passed on, and the gunman completed his slow pivot. Almost imperceptibly, Stark relaxed.

"What the blazes?" Brockton exclaimed. He was staring up at the ridge above, a shocked expression on his face.

Stark followed his gaze. The afternoon sunlight seemed to strike gold from the figure standing there amidst the rocks. Like some specter of the long dead past, sword in hand, the conquistador gazed down on the treasure hunters. Stark felt the chill of dire peril as he recognized the figure silhouetted there.

Rodriguez!

How the war chief had reached the position on the ledge undetected was of little consequence now. What mattered was why he was there at all.

"Don't shoot!" Brockton commanded his men, as more of them became aware of the bizarre figure standing motionless above them. "Cover me," he told Hawk, then stepped forward. "You there! Who are you?"

There was no reply.

"Try Spanish," Hawk suggested, his hand hovering near the .45.

Brockton repeated his query in fluent Spanish, then added, "Where are you from? Answer me."

"You are seeking a man and two women," Rodriguez called out at last in response.

Brockton advanced another step. "Yes, can you help me?" Clearly he was willing to play along with this stranger, whatever his origins might be.

Stark suspected Brockton would've dealt with the devil himself if it meant locating the treasure and getting revenge for the gunshot he'd suffered at the same time.

"I can see that you find these people," Rodriguez asserted. "But it must be on my terms."

A sickness churned deep in Stark's gut as he listened to a madman betray his people. For despite whatever precautions Rodriguez might insist upon, he wouldn't be able to control Brockton once the connection between the conquistadors and the gold became evident. And Brockton was probably realizing that connection even now.

"Come down here and we'll talk," Brockton offered congenially.

"No! I will not place myself in your power. I will give you directions to follow, and I will meet you there when you reach the location I designate." His voice rolled on after that, giving directions that would lead Brockton and his men to the proximity of the treasure cave.

Stark realized bitterly that he should have expected this. Instead of initiating an attack on the intruders, Rodriguez's jealousy had led him to play Judas. He had elected to ally himself with the enemy to gain vengeance against the prisoner who had usurped his power and the captain who had betrayed the gods he had served all his life. Ultimately, Stark knew, Captain Mendoza himself, along with the gold and the other conquistadors, would be offered up on the alter of the war chief's madness.

But there was a devious cunning to Rodriguez's refusal to fall into the clutches of Brockton and his men. "I can have some of the boys try to slip up behind him," Hawk whispered.

"No," Brockton responded. "He'd spot such a move in a minute and disappear. Whoever he is, he moves like a blamed ghost."

"I'm sure I can drop him from here before he can move," Hawk insisted. "I won't kill him. I'll just put a slug in his leg."

"Too risky," Brockton decided. "For now we'll have to go along with what he wants us to do."

Stark had heard enough. While the treasure hunters' attention was fixed on Rodriguez, he motioned Escobar to a silent retreat. The younger man's face bore an expression of shocked disbelief at what they had heard, but he still moved with superb skill as they withdrew. By the time they halted, Rodriguez had disappeared and Brockton was excitedly barking orders to get under way.

"Go back to the outpost," Stark instructed his guide. "Tell the captain what you have seen and heard here. Tell him to prepare for war."

"But what of you?" Escobar queried. "Where do you go?"

"I'm going after Rodriguez," Stark said with deadly calm.

Chapter Fourteen

There was a chance, Stark thought, that he could still prevent Brockton from finding the cave by preventing further contact between Rodriguez and the treasure hunters.

It had been years since he had hunted human prey in these hills, he reflected wryly as he moved cautiously over the terrain. Had it been Rodriguez who had fired on him earlier with a crossbow? If so, he was doing now what he had refused to do then—going after the enemy on the enemy's own ground.

The lengthening shadows signaled that it was growing late in the day. If he didn't finish this soon, darkness would descend on the hills and cast the odds even more in Rodriguez's favor. He didn't want to kill the war chief, but he guessed he would have no choice. Rodriguez wouldn't allow himself to be captured, and Stark doubted he could even get close enough to the wily conquistador to make that possible. Likely he'd have to fire on the man from some distance to bring him down. And he didn't relish the use of a gun so close to Brockton's army. A single gunshot would alert them to his presence and even his identity.

Still, there seemed no viable alternative.

He had crossed the draw well behind the advancing column of men, and made his way stealthily along the ridge toward the place where Rodriguez had shown himself. As he figured, he found no evidence that the war chief had ever occupied the spot. He crouched among the boulders and considered his alternatives.

Rodriguez might well expect Brockton to send men after him. Thus he would probably plan for a possible pursuit and not parallel the column's route for the time being. Likely he would leave the ridge and take the safest trail to the rendezvous point he had designated to Brockton.

Stark's eyes were drawn to a line of evergreens that ran from the ridge into a sheltered draw, and from there into a shallow canyon. The trees would have provided concealment for Rodriguez as he left the ridge. Stark cautiously worked his way from tree to tree. The conifers were not set particularly close, but their canopy blocked much of the fading daylight. He saw nothing among the shadows, and with shotgun at the ready, he moved as rapidly as he dared.

A larger stand of evergreens, several acres in area, spread along the sides of the shallow canyon. Somewhere in those emerald shadows, Rodriguez might lurk even now. As that disturbing thought came to him, he saw a metallic gleam among the ground cover in front of him. He brought his rifle to bear and stared intently. He could make out the prone form of a man partially concealed in the underbrush.

His finger tightened on the trigger, and he studied the figure intently as his eyes adjusted to the gloom. The man lay on his back, arms outflung, and something told Stark that whoever it was was dead.

Stark eased forward, staying low, and found himself staring into the lifeless eyes of one of the conquistadors. The man's throat had been neatly slit right above the edge of his armor. He hadn't been dead much over an hour, Stark guessed.

He remembered his own earlier thoughts about a second scout assigned by Mendoza to keep tabs on the treasure hunters. This, then, must be that scout. Rather than be observed in his treason, Rodriguez had ruthlessly disposed of his own comrade and left him here partially concealed in the brush.

A troubling thought goaded Stark as he turned to go. *Why only partially concealed?*

As the probable answer came to him, he flung himself sidewise and down in that same instant. A sharp point of wind hissed past his ear followed by a small thud of impact. He didn't need to look at the missile to know a crossbow shaft vibrated in the trunk of the tree behind him.

Rodriguez had cleverly been waiting in ambush for anyone who followed him. He had deliberately left the body in view to lure his pursuer into a vulnerable position. The cold cunning of the plan chilled Stark as he scanned the evergreens around him, resisting the urge to pump shells blindly into the woods in the direction from which the bolt had come.

He saw nothing, and Brockton's words floated into his mind. Rodriguez did indeed move like a ghost.

No more bolts were immediately forthcoming. Stark lay still, hoping Rodriguez would think his single shot had struck home. He doubted the war chief would be so easily fooled, but he also doubted Rodriguez would want to remain very long in one spot in case Stark had not come alone.

A minute passed, then another. Stark almost missed the faint suggestion of movement slightly below him. It was gone before he could bring his shotgun to bear, but he knew he had glimpsed his foe. He also knew Rodriguez hadn't fired on him from that point. The angle and trajectory were wrong, which meant that even under his concentrated scrutiny, the war chief had been able to move a significant distance without being detected.

Stark knew he must shift positions too. Rodriguez undoubtedly had his location pinpointed now. Some yards to his left was a dry ditch, not much over two feet in depth, which served as a natural drainage channel for rainwater. He writhed his way to it and slipped over the side. By staying flat on his belly, he had adequate cover to descend the ridge.

As the ditch petered out, Stark eased to his feet behind a thick evergreen. He was acutely aware that his quarry might be close at hand anywhere within a three hundred-sixty degree radius. Or if Rodriguez had chosen flight, he might be long gone from the vicinity.

He detected no betraying motion as he peered about carefully. He couldn't stay where he was forever. He made a swift darting rush to another tree, and another after that, pausing there to get his bearings. Still no sight or sound to indicate Rodriguez's presence. He catfooted forward, careful to move silently, all his senses alert as he stayed to the edge of the trees and the cover they offered.

Then he came across the first sign of the war chief's passage. A partial footprint was visible in a patch of sand before the ground dropped away into a maze of gullies and boulders.

Stark paused to study the print. It was only partial

and might well have been made in a careless moment by a man hurrying to reach the rough terrain beyond. It was the kind of mistake even a skilled woodsman might make while moving fast to evade an enemy.

But not Rodriguez.

Stark knew deep down in his gut that Rodriguez was again trying to lure him into an ambush. Carefully, very carefully, he began to withdraw.

This time the crossbow bolt whispered past more than two feet wide to be lost in the woods. Stark dropped and rolled, aware that Rodriguez had shown evidence of his volatile anger for the first time in the stalk. Realizing that Stark wasn't going to fall for the trap, the war chief had fired anyway at a poor target. Stark's ability to anticipate his ambushes were obviously beginning to gnaw at his mercurial nature.

Once more, Stark refused to return fire. He lay in the shadows beneath the trees, and after a time realized he now knew how to take Rodriguez.

So far he had been playing the war chief's game—allowing Rodriguez to choose the sites of confrontation. It was not a game he could hope to play successfully for very long. Ultimately, one of the traps would catch him.

Far better to force the war chief to come to him. He was certain Rodriguez had identified him by now. And he was equally certain the conquistador's maniacal hatred of him would goad the man into coming after him if he gave up the pursuit.

From here on, Stark decided, the game would be played on *his* terms.

Staying within the edge of the trees, he retreated along the ridge. When he was sure he was out of crossbow range, he moved into the open, running hard for the cover of broken ground. Rodriguez was certain to see him fleeing, and the man would follow.

As the shadows lengthened, Stark worked his way across the rutted terrain, skirting the base of a large hill, careful not to stay exposed for very long, but careful also to make himself occasionally visible. Even if Rodriguez guessed what he was doing, Stark was betting the man's fanatical hatred wouldn't allow him to give up the chase.

It came as somewhat of a shock—so closely did Stark feel his mind linked to his enemy's—when he realized he had not yet clearly seen Rodriguez since the hunt began.

He dropped down the precipitous side of a canyon in a series of controlled falls, and paused once he reached the canyon floor. The area looked familiar. Careful to stay close to the steep wall, he followed the course of the canyon and came to the site he expected. His journey with Escobar, the convoluted stalk, had combined to bring him to the rock overhang with its ancient cave drawings where he, Prudence, and Sarah had spent the night. As an ambush site, it was ideal.

Rodriguez would certainly find him, of that he had no doubt. He had left enough of a trail to lure him on. It now remained only to make preparations to receive him.

At the back of the overhang, in among the shadows, Stark lay flat on his belly, facing the mouth of the near-cave. Anyone entering would be clearly silhouetted, and in the gathering dusk, he would be almost invisible. It would be impossible for Rodriguez to pick him off with the crossbow from outside the cave. The war chief would be forced to come inside, placing himself in the crosshairs of Stark's shotgun.

He cradled the heavy repeater, butt against his cheek, barrel covering the entrance. His Colt Peacemaker he placed on the sand, ready to be snatched up. He didn't think he would need the handgun. Rodriguez shouldn't be able to get ten feet under the overhang before the shotgun stopped him cold.

Stretched prone, rifle at the ready, Stark waited.

After a time he had to fight the urge to turn and make sure he wasn't being menaced from behind—perhaps by the ghost of whatever ancient artist had created the hunting scenes on the wall. He remembered the way the animals and hunters had seemed to move in mythical rhythm beneath the flickering lantern light.

Somewhere an owl called, a harbinger of the night. Stark forced all distracting thoughts from his mind. The entryway remained clear, although darkness was gathering fast. He battled the sudden urge to yawn. He was thirsty and his knees and back ached from lying stiff and still for so long. For the first time he realized how tired he was from the day's exertions, and he felt the heaviness of his eyelids.

Suddenly with no warning, a figure rose up unexpectedly before him, like a specter bursting forth from the grave.

One moment he was gazing down the gunbarrel. The next, the armored figure was upon him, wild battle cry shocking his nerves to immobility, naked sword slashing down at his skull.

Reflexes saved him. The reflexes of a man who had lived too long hunting others to ever lose that razor's edge of quickness that could spell the difference between life and death. Somehow he got the shotgun up crosswise above him as he rolled, feeling the blade chop into the butt only inches above his face.

Rodriguez's blade bit into the wood and held there. Stark tried to twist the shotgun and pull the sword from his opponent's hands. But the war chief hauled back, and the gun was wrenched from Stark's unprepared grip.

Then the sword was free, seeming to flash as it lifted and cut down. Stark rolled desperately. The shotgun was gone, the revolver lost somewhere in the sand. He scrambled wildly to his knees as the armored figure loomed over him. He saw the maniacal visage of Rodriguez, saw the sword slashing down.

Then his hand closed about the hilt of the ancient sword half buried in the sand. He snatched it up. Blade to blade, the clash of metal echoed from the rock walls.

The unexpected counter threw Rodriguez off balance, his footing uncertain in the sand. Stark shoved hard against him, sending him staggering back. Then Stark was on his feet, gripping the broken sword desperately in his fist.

Stark still couldn't quite grasp how Rodriguez had managed to get within sword range of him without being detected. But the fact remained that he had. And now Stark faced a better armed, more highly skilled opponent in a duel to the death.

Rodriguez recovered quickly. He held his sword extended slightly, making small circling motions with its tip. "I will kill you, blasphemer," he hissed.

To Stark it seemed he confronted a demon from hell. Without warning, Rodriguez lunged, his body leaning into the move, arm straightening as he thrust. Stark was no swordsman, but he was bigger and stronger than Rodriguez, and he had fought many times with a knife. He batted the darting blade aside with his own shorter weapon, and suddenly the disadvantage didn't matter. He had a weapon in his hand, and his enemy stood before him.

Rodriguez faltered at the grim determination on his face.

But only for an instant. The war chief attacked savagely, edging forward, his side to Stark, sword darting and jabbing like the tongue of a serpent. Stark parried and parried again, careful not to let his movements carry his own short blade too wide to allow time to recover.

He tried to circle and come in from the side, but Rodriguez only shifted stances and lunged again, driving him back. He sidestepped, fast in the sand, and thrust hard himself. The jagged point of the old sword landed under Rodriguez's arm and glanced harmlessly off the war chief's armor. Stark dodged frantically back as Rodriguez's blade swept toward him in a horizontal slash.

This could not go on. It was Stark's reflexes against the greater reach and skill of the armor-clad swordsman, and eventually one of the war chief's deceiving, darting movements would strike home. Stark kicked out with his booted foot at Rodriguez's blade, raising a spray of sand. Rodriguez flinched at the unorthodox move, then snarled his hatred and came in once more.

Stark kicked again, only this time he dug his toe under the battered old helmet that had been buried with the sword and sent it spinning up into Rodriguez's face.

The war chief fell back, flailing reflexively at the unidentified object in the dim light. Stark flung himself forward, thrusting up from his side with all his weight and strength. The broken jagged end of the old sword went in neatly above Rodriguez's armor, the metal biting into his throat in the exact spot where the war chief himself had inflicted the killing wound on the other conquistador.

Breathing hard, Stark stood for a time over the body of his opponent, not quite believing it was over. Finally he dropped the ancient broken sword beside the war chief and turned to retrieve his guns.

He had never encountered anyone like Rodriguez

before. The man's abilities had been uncanny. While he stared and watched and waited, Rodriguez had crept to within scant feet of him without being detected.

He was lucky—no, blessed—to have survived the madman's attack.

It was fully dark by the time he buried the dead war chief in a crevice on the canyon floor. The owl called hauntingly again. It wouldn't be easy traveling by night, but he felt a driving need to do so.

He had underestimated Rodriguez. He might well have done the same with Brockton. He knew now that killing Rodriguez wouldn't prevent Brockton from finding the treasure cave.

The man was as madly committed to his cause as Rodriguez had been to his. Rodriguez's directions would take Brockton too close to the Cave with the Iron Door. When the war chief didn't appear, Brockton would surely set his men to combing the entire area. It would only be a matter of time before he located the cave . . . and its guardians.

And Prudence and the others as well.

Chapter Fifteen

It took Stark most of the night traveling over unfamiliar terrain to return to the outpost. Even knowing where he was when he left the rock overhang, he had experienced a frantic time of disorientation. When he reached the vicinity of the treasure cave, he had been unable to immediately locate it in the predawn blackness. It was easy to understand why some treasure hunters, even having seen the iron door, couldn't return to it later.

Mendoza was waiting for him when he arrived, and it was clear the man had spent another troubled night. Pain registered on his aristocratic features as Stark described the treachery of Rodriguez and the man's murder of one of his brethren.

"Escobar told me that Rodriguez had given the intruders directions to our canyon." The old man sighed wearily. "Even in death he accomplishes his plans. We will now have to fight this army." He sighed again. "You are very tired, senor. You must rest while I think on all you have told me. I will send for you shortly."

Stark nodded. Mendoza was right. He desperately needed a few hours sleep, or he would be no good to anyone. Besides, he was anxious to check on Prudence and the others.

Rankin and Sarah were sleeping soundly, but Prudence awoke when he entered the large room. In hushed tones he told her all that had happened, then fell into an exhausted slumber. When he surfaced again he knew it must be shortly after dawn.

Mendoza summoned him even before he'd finished his meager breakfast. The old captain regarded him stoically across the massive table desk. "I have decided. You and the others are free to go. In killing Rodriguez you have done more than enough to win your freedom. One of my men will show you an alternate route out of the canyon. You can leave before the intruders arrive."

Stark was deeply touched. He knew the struggle the man had faced to reach this point. Without them and their weapons, the conquistadors were doomed for sure. "Thank you. I appreciate the offer, and I accept on behalf of my wife and my friends. But I choose to stay and fight with you and your men."

Mendoza appeared sincerely puzzled. "But why? This is not your battle. What do you hope to gain? I have sensed from the first that you care nothing for the gold."

"Nor do you," Stark said with conviction. "We both fight for things that have more meaning."

Stark had thought long and hard about the old conquistador on his way back in the darkness, and he had realized they had much in common. They were both warriors. Mendoza had recognized that fact first, and had commented on it in his office before Stark had left with Escobar to view Brockton's war party.

As he'd considered the matter further, Stark had seen other similarities as well. They both lived by a warrior's code of duty which crossed timelines and cultures. And like good warriors down through the ages, Mendoza had acted only out of duty in protecting the gold. Not avarice. Not greed. Not vengeance on the innocent.

But in offering to release them, Mendoza had surpassed duty and gone on to a level above.

Stark had responded in kind by refusing to leave.

When Mendoza continued to stare at him in puzzlement, Stark explained. "I fight against the evil of the intruders . . . and I fight for a friend."

The man seemed staggered by his words. "I am that friend?"

Stark nodded, and the old man turned quickly away.

"I'll go tell my wife and the others to prepare to leave," Stark said brusquely. "Then I'll return so we can make battle plans."

"You can't send me away, James Stark!" Prudence cried angrily when he told her of Mendoza's offer. "I'm staying if you are. You know that."

Timothy Rankin didn't sound quite as passionate, but after a glance at Sarah, he spoke up as well. "We'll stay too. Unless we defeat Brockton here, he'll just keep coming after us. I'd rather die putting up a fight against him than as a helpless victim of his torture and abuse."

Their decision to stay gave Stark the same surge of emotion that Mendoza must have felt at his own offer. He'd expected as much from Prudence, but not from Rankin and Sarah. He felt a new respect for the young professor.

Stark choked down the lump in his throat. "Then we better get back to Mendoza and lay our plans. Hopefully they've got our horses and supplies stashed nearby. We need our spare ammunition."

* * *

Once again Stark crouched above a canyon and waited for Brockton and his men. The mid-morning sun was already warm, but its rays felt good on the back of his neck.

He glanced over at Prudence beside him, armed with her Winchester. She felt his gaze and turned to give him a tight little grin that betrayed the tension they were all under. He didn't like her being a part of this. Nor did he like the presence of Timothy and Sarah beyond her. But they needed every gun and crossbow available. Their total number was only fourteen, allowing for the deaths of Rodriguez and his victim.

Brockton and his men outnumbered them two to one—and were all heavily armed. It wouldn't be an easy battle, and victory was anything but assured. But Stark had chosen this site carefully from among those Mendoza had shown him. Here the distance to the canyon floor was perfect. The range of the crossbows would be as deadly as any rifle.

The conquistadors would all be in place now, scattered among the rocks and ledges along both sides of the canyon wall. The iron door was out of sight on down the canyon. Though Stark couldn't see any of the primitive warriors on the far side, he knew they were over there somewhere waiting for the column to appear so they could begin the attack.

"We'll use one of your men to lure them into the canyon," he'd told Mendoza. "They'll believe it's Rodriguez as long as he keeps his distance." He had decided it was better to carry the fight to their enemies rather than wait to be discovered. "I'll give them a chance to surrender, and if they don't we'll open fire."

Mendoza appeared ready to question the wisdom of giving armed enemies a chance. Then as he studied Stark's face, he nodded. "I understand. It wouldn't be right to kill them without offering quarter." No more was said on the subject of warnings as preparations were quickly made.

Four guns and ten crossbows against over twenty-five experienced fighting men. Not the best of odds. But the element of surprise was theirs, and the site was to their advantage. The straight stretch of canyon would allow the entire column to be seen at one time.

The canyon walls on either side were rugged and studded with boulders and outcroppings offering good cover. And while it was possible for an active man to climb up, it would be impossible for a horseman. The only viable escape for Brockton and his men was back the way they had come. And even that route wouldn't be as easy as it looked.

An armored figure appeared in the canyon coming from the same direction as the approaching column of riders. The figure waved in signal, then vanished into the cliff face. It was Escobar who had volunteered to appear before the intruders and lure them in. The column was only moments behind him.

Stark fingered the lever-action shotgun and offered up a wordless prayer. He was stationed at the far end of the ambush site from where Brockton's men would enter. By the time the lead riders had reached his position, the entire force should be visible and vulnerable. He glanced over at Prudence and was touched by the sheer determination and courage on her face. He thought again how lucky he was to have found her.

The sound of shod hooves on stone drew his attention back to the canyon floor. Douglas Brockton and Milo Hawk still rode alertly at the head of their small army. Less prudent men might have come in at a gallop, but Brockton kept the pace at a walk. His head, like that of his gunslinger's, turned to scan for signs of danger. Recalling Milo Hawk's uncanny sixth sense at being watched, Stark held his breath.

He was aware in that intense moment of the sun warm on his neck, the wood and metal of the Winchester in his grip, the hardness of the stone beneath his knee, Prudence's nervous excited presence beside him.

As the tail end of the column came fully into view and Brockton and Hawk drew abreast of his position, Stark called out his offer of surrender. "Brockton, you're under the gun! Surrender! You don't have a chance!"

But Brockton and Hawk were already coming off their horses on the inside, so the animals' bulk would serve to protect them. As Hawk's feet hit the ground, his gun was in his hand, blasting up at the spot from which Stark had called. The slug whined off rock near Stark's head—an incredible snap shot.

Brockton, hampered some by his injured arm, was off his horse just an instant behind Hawk. He fumbled in his saddlebag as a cloud of crossbow bolts rained down.

So much for warnings, Stark thought, and jammed the butt of the shotgun against his shoulder. Brockton and Hawk were protected by their horses, but the next pair of riders in line were still struggling to dismount. The shotgun kicked against Stark's shoulder and the nearest man pirouetted out of his saddle. At the same instant his companion slumped sidewise as a crossbow bolt buried itself in his chest.

Stark fired and fired again at the pandemonium of yelling men and panicked horses which had erupted below. He was conscious of Prudence, Sarah, and Timothy adding their guns to his.

The first volley of shots had been devastating. A

third of Brockton's men were down, most from crossbow bolts. Attacking from ambush, wielding their weapons with brutal efficiency, Mendoza's conquistadors were in the element for which training and heritage had superbly equipped them.

A few of the men who had survived were wisely riding hard back the way they'd come. Stark doubted that they'd return to the battle. The rest were dismounting and scrambling for cover, throwing wild shots at their unseen assailants.

Stark shifted his attention to Brockton. Hawk was doing his job well, aiming now with cool efficiency, laying down a field of fire to cover his boss. As Stark watched, Brockton drew back his arm and flung something arcing up at the canyon wall. Stark had only a glimpse of the oblong object with its sputtering fuse as it flew toward him.

"Get down!" he shouted, throwing himself atop Prudence.

The missile struck the cliff somewhere below them, and the blast literally shook the ledge on which they crouched. A shower of small stones pummeled Stark's back, and his ears rang as he lifted his head.

Obviously in his preparations for treasure hunting, Brockton had included a supply of dynamite.

Another explosion erupted from the far wall of the canyon and Stark glimpsed two armored bodies tumbling earthward. Brockton continued to throw sticks of dynamite alternately at each wall, and under cover of the explosions he and Hawk were moving on foot up the canyon toward the treasure vault. Stark saw that he carried the saddlebag of explosives with him, and wondered how much of the stuff the maniac had brought.

Stark raised his gun and fired, but he was too late. The pair disappeared around a turn in the wall.

"Jim, don't go after him!" Prudence cried grabbing at his arm.

He wrenched free. "I have to! This will never be over if he gets away!" He sprang from concealment and scrambled down the cliff face in pursuit.

As he reached the canyon floor, he glimpsed a snarling unshaven face bringing a sixgun to bear on him from behind a boulder. Stark fired his shotgun from the hip, its blast mingling with that of the gunman's revolver. The unshaven man convulsed back against the boulder as an impact all but wrenched the shotgun from Stark's grip. The man's single shot had glanced off the gun, smashing its mechanism. Stark flung it aside, conscious of the vicious battle raging all around him, and raced on in pursuit of Brockton and Hawk.

He quickly lost track of them in the jumble of boulders which studded the narrow canyon floor beyond the ambush site. Up ahead he spotted the iron door to the treasure vault. His nerves pulled tight, for the door stood open. He knew Brockton must be inside transfixed by the gold.

Suddenly Milo Hawk stepped out from behind a jagged outcropping to bar the path some fifteen feet in front of him.

The gunfighter was disheveled, his clothes dusty, but that air of violent arrogance still emanated from him. He stood erect, feet close together, arms hanging loosely at his sides. His holstered gun had never seemed more a part of his total being. The harsh planes of his features split in a hideous grin.

The face of evil, Stark thought.

"I expected you might be along, Stark," Hawk said easily, with a wild excitement underlying his tone. "At any rate, I was hoping you'd be. What in blazes did we get into back there?"

Stark faced him, his own stance not so much different from Hawk's. "The Golden Ones. They guard the treasure."

Hawk sneered. "Don't tell me fairytales, Stark. But the treasure, does it exist?"

"It's real enough to cost you your life if you let it."

The gunman's chuckle had a mocking ring. "Well, I reckon I'll just go take a look at it when I finish my business with you."

"We don't have any business."

That dark fire flared in Hawk's cold eyes, and his nostrils distended as though he were scenting prey. "You're wrong, Stark. I've wanted this chance at you ever since I heard you were on this job. Now I've got it."

"You should have listened to Brockton," Stark warned.

For an instant Hawk looked perplexed. But only for an instant. Then, with no warning, his hand moved and his gun was clear of leather.

Stark's shot caught him in the chest, left of center— a heart shot that drove him dancing back on his heels, his revolver blasting its discharge into the earth at his feet. A stunned look froze on his face as he went sprawling to the ground. Stark lowered his smoking gun and crossed to the fallen gunman. The dark fire had faded from Hawk's staring eyes. He was dead.

"You should have listened to Brockton," Stark repeated. "He told you not to give me a chance."

"Milo never was real good at taking advice. I suspected right along that that might be his downfall."

Stark tensed as Douglas Brockton's cultured voice sounded close behind him.

"Don't even think of trying to pull anything, Stark," Brockton warned. "I have my gun out and it's pointed square at your back. And for sure I won't be the fool

Milo was. I'll shoot you down where you stand. Now, toss your sixgun away."

Stark knew he had no choice. Brockton had him in a dead drop. Slowly he let the Colt Peacemaker slide from his fingers. Then he turned to face his captor.

Brockton's handsome face was set in a mocking grin. "Well, well, here I was needing some help carrying all that gold out of the cave, and you show up. This has to be my lucky day."

Stark glanced up at the still open iron door. "So you've been inside, huh? I'm surprised you were able to tear yourself away."

Brockton laughed crudely. "It was hard, believe me. But one has to be practical. Like Hawk, I knew you would be coming along, and I wanted to be ready for you."

Stark looked past Brockton toward the site of the battle. Without the aid of the explosives, the gunfire of the invaders was dying swiftly away. The unmistakable sound of other riders fleeing down the canyon drifted to them on the wind.

"Give it up, Brockton," he advised. "Your pet gunsnake is dead. And from the sounds of it, most of your army has turned tail and run. Face facts. You've lost the battle."

"Not as long as I have you. Your friends will do anything I ask to keep me from putting a bullet in you. When they arrive, I'll have them round up a few riderless horses and load up the saddlebags with gold bars. I've seen it, Stark. Even the little I can carry with me will allow me to live like a king for the rest of my life. I'll take you along, of course, to ensure I have safe passage. And once we leave these mountains behind, I'll figure out some way to get even for that bullet you put in my shoulder."

"The gold is not yours to take!" a haunting voice called shrilly in Spanish. "We guard the gold for the gods!"

Stark and Brockton whirled in unison to see Mendoza, resplendent in full armor, standing beside the open iron door. In one hand he held a lighted torch. In the other the saddlebag full of explosives Brockton had carried into the cave. A long piece of cord was hanging out of the flap of the saddlebag, and Mendoza was moving the torch ever closer to that dangling fuse.

"No!" Brockton cried in his fluid Spanish. "There's enough dynamite in that bag to bring down this whole mountain! What do you want?"

"Let that one go," Mendoza demanded imperially, "and we will speak about terms."

"So that's it," Brockton hissed in English to Stark. "That lunatic is just running a bluff to try and get me to release you. Well, it won't work! You know me, Stark. I can drill you and still drop him before he lights that fuse. Now tell him to call it off, or I'll kill you both right now."

"Captain Mendoza!" Stark called. "This one is evil! He will kill us both to have the gold! He instructs me to tell you to put down the torch!"

"I know he is evil," Mendoza replied calmly. "The gold only attracts evil men. So it has been down through the ages. Perhaps it is time to bring the evil to an end." With that he very deliberately moved the torch toward the fuse.

"No!" Brockton screamed, shooting wildly.

Despite the golden armor, every shot found home in the aged conquistador's body. But drawing on a super-human strength, Mendoza lit the fuse as he was falling and hurled the saddlebag full of explosives deep into the cave.

Stark hit the ground rolling at Brockton's first shot, and came up with the Colt Peacemaker in his hand. When Brockton turned the gun on him, he was ready. He drilled the treasure hunter square in the chest just as the sound of a mammoth explosion shook the ground beneath his feet.

The force of the blast hurled Mendoza off the ledge to land within a few feet of Stark and the fallen Brockton. Stark ran to the old man and hefted the body over his shoulder as the first stones of the massive avalanche rained down from above. He ran furiously back up the canyon, fighting for breath in the dust and silt that swirled out in a blinding, choking storm.

He rounded a bend in the canyon wall, and dropped to his knees in the shelter of an outcropping that blocked most of the flying debris. Still breathing hard, he lowered the old man's body carefully to the ground.

Surprisingly, Mendoza's eyes flickered open and he smiled weakly up at Stark. "You are unhurt?"

Stark nodded. "Don't talk," he panted. "Save your breath."

"No need," the old man rasped, "for soon I will speak no more." He smiled again. "It seems Rodriguez got his wishes after all. The gold is safe from the intruders."

Stark felt an overwhelming sadness. Mendoza was obviously dying, and his thoughts were still on his duty to protect the gold. "You shouldn't have risked your life for the gold. It wasn't worth it."

"Oh, I know," Mendoza chided gently. "I did not risk my life for the gold. I risked my life for a friend . . ."

His eyelids slowly fluttered shut, and a calm expression settled on his features. Stark swallowed hard. Maybe the old warrior would find a peace in death that had eluded him in life.

Stark stood to his feet. His eyes were stinging fiercely, and it wasn't only from the dust he'd passed through. He knew without a doubt now that Mendoza had drawn Brockton's fire to give him a chance to recover his gun.

He fought down the surge of emotion that swept over him at the thought of Mendoza's sacrifice. He turned almost angrily as the dust was settling, and stared back toward the site of the explosion. A huge pile of rubble lay where the treasure cave had been.

Of the iron door there was no sign.

Chapter Sixteen

"We will leave this place," Escobar said, almost with a sense of release. "There is nothing left for us here."

He stood with Stark and the others on the rim of the sheltered box canyon where their horses had been turned loose to graze after their capture.

Stark regarded the young conquistador. "Where will you go?"

Escobar shrugged and smiled slightly. "Our wives have told us of a land far to the south where the inhabitants speak our tongue. They say that the warriors of their people fled there after the white man invaded their land."

"He must mean Mexico," Prudence whispered.

Stark nodded. He knew well that many of the renegade Indian leaders had escaped across the border rather than be consigned to life on the reservations. He thought of the rugged mountains of southern Mexico and Guatemala, and acknowledged that perhaps that would be a good refuge for these men who had been born so far out of their time.

"There are not many of us left," Escobar continued. Sadness tinged his words.

Again Stark nodded, recalling the aftermath of the battle. Three conquistadors had fallen besides Mendoza. The small band had had their number cut in half in only a matter of days.

But they had proven themselves valiant warriors to the end.

He had returned to the battle after the explosion, to find it all but over. When he called out his second offer of surrender, the remaining invaders had quickly taken him up on it.

Brockton's gunmen who survived the ambush had been allowed to leave. Stark doubted they'd ever return or that anyone would believe their stories of what had transpired. In a few years, their tales would be only another chapter in the mysterious legend of the Lost Cave with the Iron Door.

It really made no difference, however, whether they were believed or not. The cave and its iron door and its gold were gone, buried beneath tons of stone and rubble brought down by that final explosion. Douglas Brockton had finally found the gold he lusted after, and another set of bones could be counted among those who had died for the treasure.

"You'll find your supplies and saddles in a cave by that tree on the floor of the canyon," Escobar said pointing. "There is a passageway out at the far end. You will just need to remove the crossbars we put in place to keep the horses confined."

"Is there anything we can do for you before we go?" Stark asked.

The young man smiled teasingly over at Prudence. "You might remember us to the God whom you say is more interested in His children than in treasure and gold."

Prudence laughed genuinely. To Stark, it was a good

sound to hear after all the danger and uncertainty they'd endured since this treasure hunt had begun.

"I'll do that," Prudence said, offering her hand to Escobar.

He shook it and then reached out in turn to Stark. "You are a great warrior, senor. It was an honor to fight beside you."

Stark clasped the man's hand firmly. "The honor was mine." He hesitated. "Might I give you a word of advice, Escobar?"

"Certainly, senor."

"Your party might find traveling easier and less dangerous if you dress more as men do today."

Escobar reached up and removed the odd helmet. He looked at it long and hard. He must realize, Stark knew, that he'd be trading safety for the one thing that had given identity and purpose to his life. It was surely a hard choice to make, but necessary in order for the small band to move into the future.

"You are of course right, senor. We will appropriate clothing from the fallen intruders before we bury them. Their horses, too, will serve us well as we make our journey."

Stark nodded a final time. This parting was one of the most difficult he could remember. He hated to consider the hardships these throwbacks would face in trying to carve out a place for themselves in the present world. He had to force himself to think only of their warrior spirits and dauntless courage.

"Vaya con Dios, mi amigo," he said simply. "Go with God."

Escobar's eyes grew warm. "You also, senor."

They watched him make his way back down the meandering trail they had followed to this pasture and their horses. All of them remained silent until he was well out of sight.

"Do you think they'll make it to Mexico?" Sarah asked tentatively, holding tight to her fiance's arm, as if for reassurance.

"I do," Prudence said emphatically. "They're made of stern stuff to have survived in this harsh unforgiving place. It won't be easy, but they'll make it all right."

Timothy Rankin patted Sarah's hand where it rested on his arm. "You know, it's strange that I even care what happens to them, considering all they put me through. But I actually wish them every good fortune. And I'm voting with Prudence. From what I've seen of them, they'll be fine."

Stark found Rankin's words encouraging. After all, the young professor had observed more of the conquistadors' adaptive qualities than anyone.

But apparently now Timothy was ready to leave the whole experience behind. "Well, Mr. Stark, do you think you can lead us out of this rock-strewn wilderness and back to civilization? I've got a learned thesis to write about the conquistadors in the new world."

"Timothy," Sara chided. "I thought you said none of that was important anymore."

"I'm joking," Rankin said, smiling down on her. "However, I'll admit it *is* hard to give up on the project that kept me sane during all those months sitting alone in that dark cell. But more than anyone alive, I know the evil generated by the conquistadors' gold. It's cost too many lives already. It's better just to let the legend die."

Stark admired the young professor for his noble intentions. But the legend itself would not die, of that Stark was certain. The mystery and magic of such a tale gave it an unending life of its own. Years from now weary travelers would still sometimes imagine they saw an iron door in the vagaries of shifting light and shadow cast on the canyon walls in these mountains— only to return at a later date unable to locate it or even be sure they had seen it at all.

Stark looked over at Prudence and found her smiling at him. "Well, Mrs. Stark, are you ready to head for home?"

Her smile broadened even further. "Home! There has never been a more beautiful word!"

He nodded his head in agreement and led out on the path down to the canyon floor, making plans as he walked. They'd have to put their remaining provisions into their saddlebags and give the packhorse to Timothy to ride. But after all they'd been through, that seemed a very minor problem.

It was difficult for him to believe the transformation in their circumstances since the life and death struggle of yesterday. Their safety and freedom on this adventure had been hard won indeed. It felt good just to have survived the ordeal in one piece.

The pathway widened as they neared the bottom, and Prudence moved up beside him to slip her hand into his. He squeezed it and suddenly felt like smiling himself.